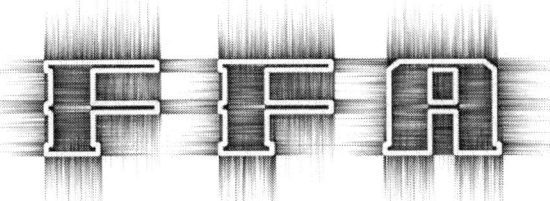

ALSO AVAILABLE FROM ZOMBIE PIRATE PUBLISHING

THE COLLAPSAR DIRECTIVE: A Science Fiction Anthology
RELATIONSHIP ADD VICE: A Thrilling Mashup of Romance and Crime
FULL METAL HORROR: A Monstrous Anthology
PHUKET TATTOO: Crazy Tales of Far Away Places
WITCHES VS WIZARDS: A Fantasy Anthology
WORLD WAR FOUR: A Science Fiction Anthology

COMING SOON

FULL METAL HORROR 2 (June 15th, 2019)
GRIEVIOUS BODILY HARM (Oct 1st, 2019)

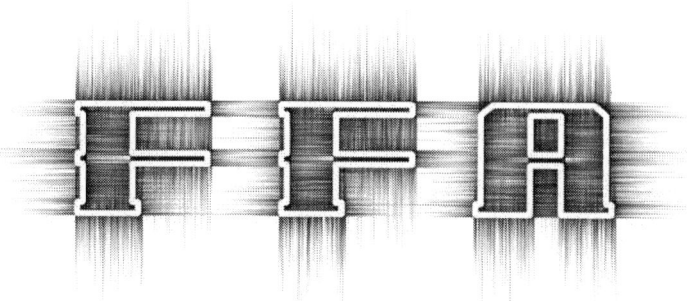

FLASH FICTION ADDICTION

Edited By
Adam Bennett and Sam M. Phillips

All characters, locations, events, and science depicted in **FLASH FICTION ADDICTION** are fictional. Any resemblance to real life locations, events, or any person living or dead is entirely coincidental.

All rights reserved. No part of this publication may be reproduced, stored in a retrieval system, or transmitted in any form or by any means, electronic, mechanical, photocopying, recording or otherwise, without the prior permission of the publishers.

The moral right of the authors has been asserted.

First Published April 2019

Cover Art by Adam Bennett and Sam M. Phillips
FLASH FICTION ADDICTION Logo by Adam Bennett
Zombie Pirate Publishing Logo by Zoe Maxwell

Flash! Ahh ahhhh!
   - Queen

CONTENTS

Foreword - pg 11
The Captain's Dinner - Shawn M. Klimek - pg 13
Beautiful Flowers - Olivia London - pg 14
Baguette - Adam Bennett - pg 18
John Smith Must Die - Mark Kuglin - pg 20
The Tally of Victory - Sam M. Phillips - pg 23
Arild's Harvest - Roy C. Booth - pg 24
Finding Terence - Rich Rurshell - pg 26
The Art of Team Building - Mel Lee Newmin - pg 31
Seth's Talks - A. L. Paradiso - pg 35
Lost Dog - Brian MacGowan - pg 37
Zero Days - Blake Jessop - pg 41
The Visitor - Michelle Perry - pg 46
854814 - Stuart West - pg 48
Gums - Daniel Craig Roche - pg 51
More Haste, Less Speed - L.T. Waterson - pg 54
The Rabbits - Clement Wilson III - pg 57
Frank the Tank - M. W. Brown - pg 61
We Named Her Olive - Alanah Andrews - pg 65
Falling - Belinda Brady - pg 67
The Flat Cap - Isabella Fox - pg 70
Harold's Last Day - Austin P. Sheehan - pg 72
The Grind - Marlon Hayes - pg 75

Serve Cold - David Bowmore - pg 78
Elsie - Jean Frost - pg 81
The Woman in the Window - Arwen West - pg 83
Hungering - Laurie Bis - pg 85
From Urn to Oak - Lozzi Counsell - pg 87
Squids aren't Monsters - Karen Thrower - pg 89
Arthur's Tale - Colin D. Palmer - pg 92
All in a Day's Work - Melanie Waghorne - pg 96
A Lover's Dwelling - Randal Eldon Green - pg 99
Growing Flowers - James Pyles - pg 103
Price of a Soul - G. Dean Manuel - pg 107
After the Fall - Mary Wallace - pg 111
Hush Little Baby - Ann Stolinsky - pg 114
Like Romeo and Juliet - S. Gepp - pg 118
Just You Wait - Kelli J Gavin - pg 119
Death Revenge - Feind Gottes - pg 120
The Pain of Responsibility - P. A. O'Neil - pg 123
A Tick of Humanity - Kari Holloway - pg 126
Michael - Justin Hunter - pg 130
Pumpkin's Purpose - Emily Fluckliger - pg 134
Bombshell - Matthew Stevens - pg 137
Kink - Brian Rosenberger - pg 140
A Mama's Love - D. M. Burdett - pg 141
The Boogeyman - C. L. Williams - pg 145

High Space - Simone Cristiano - pg 148

Death of a Head Hunter - Hákon Gunnarsson - pg 151

Beauté Folle - Amanda R. Woomer - pg 154

Passengers - Jo-Anne Russell - pg 155

We Shall Survive - John Tuttle - pg 156

Ragged Claws - Zachary Sparks - pg 159

Will - Andrew J. Lucas - pg 161

The Elephant in the Room - Lincoln Lally - pg 163

Karma's a Bitch - Hanorah Papa - pg 165

Sisters - S. B. Rhodes - pg 167

My Sweet Emily - Chris Ruland - pg 171

Bank - S. Lyle Lunt - pg 175

Thankful - J. M. Ames - pg 178

Civil Rights - Lael Braday - pg 181

Tales of a Teapot - C. H. Williams - pg 184

Once Upon a Witching Hour - Nick Morrison - pg 185

New Shoes - R. L. M. Cooper - pg 189

Prehistoric Connections - A. J. Lawdring - pg 190

Mariposa - Michael Allen Roche - pg 193

Emily - Donise Sheppard - pg 195

Anonymous - Umair Mirxa - pg 199

Cranes - David M. Donachie - pg 203

Winter - Aditya Deshmukh - pg 206

Fool on the Hill - Pam Van Allen - pg 207

Horses for Courses - Alan I'Anson - pg 211

Cinnamon - Daniel Newton - pg 215

An Empty Christmas - Nerisha Kemraj - pg 219

Desire, Duty, Deed - Kain S. Bishop - pg 221

Cleaning out the Closet - Traci Mullins - pg 223

Ashes to Ashes - Rita Kruger - pg 224

Reveling in the Storm - Martina Speranza - pg 226

Meaningless Coincidence - Nileena Sunil - pg 230

A New Day - J. W. Garrett - pg 233

Home Again - Stephanie Ayers - pg 236

Seven Breaths - Susan Reabuck - pg 239

The Riddle - Susan S. Gibbons - pg 243

Cindy - Louise O'Neill - pg 247

A Man's Heart - Suanne Kim - pg 250

The Living with It - Mike Callaghan - pg 254

Room 101 - Gregg Cunningham - pg 257

Younger by the Minute - Gabriella Balcom - pg 259

Priorities - Vince Carpini - pg 262

In the Dark - Mercedes Siler - pg 265

The Minds of Birds - B. Sharpe - pg 267

The Truth about Fairies - Sheri Velarde - pg 271

A Helpful Friend - K. M. Jenkins - pg 274

Rose - C. L. Steele - pg 278

Call Me - Martin Eastland - pg 280

Hell to Pay - Maria Papa - pg 283

The Foreigner - Tony Spencer - pg 284

Moth - Bruce Rowe - pg 287

The Squat - Veronica Love - pg 290

Don't Trust the Mermaids - J. L. Knight - pg 292

I Cannot be your Pilot - Timothy Ryan Scully - pg 294

Boarding - Pretty Pete - pg 297

    Acknowledgements - pg 299

FOREWORD

With the advent of the internet and our fast paced lifestyles, people are looking to access entertainment quickly and easily. Enter flash fiction, the perfect medium for our ever-shrinking attention spans. Short and to the point, flash fiction captures a single moment or theme, going for the jugular to distract modern audiences as they wait for the train. They are ready to use, disposable stories, and yet the best of them have the ability to stay with the reader and have an emotional impact. Achieving this is not an easy feat with only a few hundred words at the writer's disposal.

Flash fiction might have become trendy in the last couple of decades, but its beginnings date back to prehistory and appear at the origins of writing. These very short stories were originally spoken folktales, and early collections from ancient Greece and India such as *Aesop's Fables* and the *Panchatantra* were later written down. These are the basis of modern flash fiction, condensing a message to make it punchy, memorable, and accessible. Many of the world's great religions use a similar format in their holy texts to inform and teach while they entertain.

In more modern times flash fiction found a voice through American writers such as Walt Whitman, Ambrose Bierce, and Kate Chopin in the 19th century, and was continued in the early 20th century through magazines such as *Cosmopolitan*. This modern tradition gave rise to probably the first collection of flash

ZOMBIE PIRATE PUBLISHING

fiction, *Cosmopolitans: Very Short Stories*, by W. Somerset Maugham in 1936.

Since then flash fiction has become a constant in the literary world, with pieces written by many famous 20th century writers including Franz Kafka, Ernest Hemingway, and Philip K. Dick. Now the internet has raised awareness of flash fiction even further with many websites and online journals specialising in the style.

And it's a style which suits the modern mind; quick, easily accessible fiction which punches above its weight. It's very addictive for writers and readers alike and this is why we've created this amazing collection of 101 flash fiction stories from authors all around the world. The variety of tales is vast and they're fun to read whether you've a few hours or a few minutes to spare. Welcome to Flash Fiction Addiction.

Sam M. Phillips and Adam Bennett
Co-Founders
Zombie Pirate Publishing
Zombiepiratepublishing.com

The Captain's Dinner
Shawn M. Klimek

Lieutenant Renard surveyed the haggard faces of his fellow crewmen, gathered around him in the starship galley.

"That last fight took a lot out of all of us," he said, prompting weary murmurs and nods. "We lost our beloved captain. But if we stick to his daring plan, most should survive long enough to reach the colony on Vance Epsilon."

Petty Officer Daniels raised a hand. "Will there be another fight tomorrow?"

Someone groaned.

"No need for that yet," said Renard. "There are fewer of us, now, and the captain was a large man... He should last us several meals."

Beautiful Flowers
Olivia London

"Tie your shoes, Ella," Mark called as his daughter hurtled down the park path, neon pink shoelaces flying everywhere. "You're going to trip."

Ella veered left to the nearest bench. She hopped up, jostling the woman already sitting there.

"Hi, I'm Ella!" his daughter said cheerfully, giving the woman a gap-toothed grin under her heart-shaped sunglasses.

Mark smiled apologetically as he approached, but the woman's face was unreadable behind her own plain sunglasses. She tucked a curl behind her ear and smiled back at Ella.

"Hello, Ella. I'm Rose."

Ella busied herself tying her shoes while Mark tried not to stare. The woman reminded him so much of Ella's late mother it hurt. After a moment Ella gave up, sticking her foot out toward her father for help. Mark, thankful for the distraction, kneeled in the dirt to gather up the laces.

"I like your dress," she told Rose, reaching out a small hand to run over the woman's skirt. "It looks like mine!"

"Ella, don't touch," Mark scolded.

"It's quite alright, Ella," Rose said kindly.

FLASH FICTION ADDICTION

Mark glanced up from tying Ella's second shoe. Not only did their dresses look alike, but they did too with their fiery curls and freckle dusted cheeks. Anyone might assume they were a family out enjoying the nice weather. His gut clenched with longing and he ducked his head back to his task with a grimace.

"Tell me," Rose went on. "What colour is your dress?"

Ella bounced, causing the worn wood bench to dip. "Purple, with white flowers like yours."

"That sounds very pretty, Ella. And what colour is mine?"

"Blue?" she asked Rose uncertainly. "Do you not know your colours?"

"Ella," Mark said sharply as he stood, feeling guilty for allowing Ella to linger. A quiet voice in the back of his mind told him he was lingering more for himself than for Ella, but he ignored it. "I'm sorry, she can be a little forward."

Ella stared at the neat bows on her feet looking chastised.

Rose reached a hand out and tapped the bench between them before settling it reassuringly on Ella's skinny knee.

"It's okay, I like to know what colour I have on. Thank you for helping me, Ella."

"I could teach you if you like!" Ella said brightly, bolstered by Rose's kindness. "I know every colour. I learned them in Mrs Wilbur's class."

Rose laughed as Mark groaned inwardly. Parents were supposed to embarrass their kids, not the other way around. Still, Rose seemed enamoured with his impertinent little ray of sunshine and this was the first woman, besides her teacher, Ella had been interested in since her mother had passed over a year ago.

"I would love that Ella," Rose said gently. "But I'm afraid I can't learn colours because I can't see them."

"Why not?"

Rose leaned down to retrieve a thin white cane tucked beneath the bench. Mark's heart ached dully. It seemed all beautiful flowers were cut down one way or another.

"I'm blind," Rose said.

Mark held his breath, waiting for Ella's response.

"So you get to wear those sunglasses everywhere?" Ella said, voice tinged with envy. "Daddy won't let me wear mine to school."

Mark and Rose laughed together. Ella held her pout for a moment before looking pleased with herself for being funny.

"This is my daddy," she said, holding her hand out toward Mark. He stepped forward and took it. "His name is Mark."

"Hi," he said, grateful Rose couldn't see the stain on his cheeks.

"Hello, Mark," Rose smiled, ducking her head shyly.

After a long moment Rose lifted her cane and stood, auburn curls dancing around her cheeks.

"Well, I should get home."

"Do you come here every day?" Ella asked, gripping Mark's hand.

"I do," Rose nodded, using her cane to find her way back to the pavement. "I enjoy the fresh air."

"Daddy," Ella peered up at Mark. "Can we come back tomorrow?"

"I don't see why not, Ella-bella."

"Well, then I suppose I'll be seeing you again?" Rose reached a hand out toward them. After a moment of hesitation, Mark took it. It was soft and delicate, the way Lily's had been.

"Yes," he agreed with certainty. "I suppose you will."

Baguette
Adam Bennett

They call me the baguette killer, which if I'm honest with you, just makes me angry. It's not a very fear inspiring name for a serial killer. I'm here with more kills than the Zodiac Killer, more time uncaptured than BTK, and I've sent more letters filled with clues than either combined. And those boys loved to send letters. And while they have infamous names that will go down in history and terrify people for years to come, I'm stuck with 'The Baguette Killer.'

One of the only things the police have ever figured out about me is that I am a native of France. I was born in Marseilles and moved to the United States when I was only twelve. Just at the right age to become fascinated with the streak of serial killers that this fine country has.

Like many of my peers my first murder was a mess. I took my prey with little effort but when the time came to complete the deed she struggled free and I was forced to improvise. I snatched up a fallen baguette, knocked to the floor during our scuffle, and jammed it down her throat. I *was* only trying to silence her screams but I must have stuffed enough of the bread down her windpipe that her air was cut off. I don't know what would be

FLASH FICTION ADDICTION

worse: being killed with a baguette, or getting stuck trying to perfect the art.

Could I have started over? Perhaps.

Did I? Never. The first kill is always sloppy, best to have it over and done with so you can move on to the fun part: perfecting your method.

I've tried whole, sliced, frozen, fresh, stale, and hot from the oven, and yet none was much more efficient than that first fumbled attempt. Jamming handfuls of bread into the prey's open gullet is as good as it gets.

So I spice things up with a clue riddled letter sent to the Bureau after each of my kills. They crack some of them, and maybe one day I'll let them catch me; after all, part of the contract an American serial killer takes with their victims is to someday be caught. Otherwise how will Hollywood ever make a factually-adjacent film about me? There needs to be a *happy* ending.

But not today.

I'll save that for after I've had a little more fun. I *just* wish they'd come up with a better name.

John Smith Must Die
Mark Kuglin

The disappearance and eventual death of the first John Smith went virtually unnoticed. It wasn't until the same fate happened to five other John Smiths that the public began to clamour—in assembled groups and in print. Outwardly, they were enraged and demanded answers, while inwardly, they cowered in fear and did everything imaginable to conceal their own beloved John Smiths.

Deathly afraid citizens installed intricate burglar alarms, assigned night watchmen, or took turns on guard duty. However, all of these efforts were—for the most part—in vain. It didn't matter how well they disguised their particular John Smith or how cleverly they hid them. Eventually, they were found.

What troubled people the most was that it was happening—despite watchful eyes— under the cloak of darkness and that the authorities seemed unable to stop it. And despite everyone's best efforts the pattern continued unabated.

Intense fear quickly turned to full on panic. Vigilante groups formed and roamed the streets. It wasn't until a near state of anarchy existed that the Supreme Council decided to act. In response, they issued Supreme Council Edit 4077. However, it had the exact opposite effect than the one they had intended. It's issuance only added to the growing maelstrom.

It simply stated, 'There is nothing to fear. For public safety, we have assigned elite teams to eliminate each and every John Smith. Anyone caught hindering the process will be dealt with severely.'

Normally, all Supreme Council Edicts were followed without question. However, this one—with its ominous warning—elicited rage and pit family and friends against one another. The disaffected were calling for an end to the Council while supporters were heard shouting back: Have you gone mad? Who are you to disagree with the Supreme Council?

* * *

Nelson Ryland sat morosely in his office re-reading Supreme Council Edict 4077 for the fourth time. Each time he did, he felt his bile rise. And for the first time in his career, he seriously considered disobeying his direct orders.

His reverie was broken when his supervisor stopped in his doorway and asked, "Have you eliminated the John Smiths we picked up last night?"

For a moment, Nelson was stunned and wasn't sure how to respond. A part of him wanted to join the protesters and the other was afraid of incurring his supervisor's wrath. However, after pausing a moment to gather his courage, he respectfully asked, "Are you sure we're doing the right thing?"

Instantly, Nelson's supervisor charged his desk—like an enraged bull elephant—and snapped back, "Have you gone mad? It's the order of the Supreme Council and it's your duty to carry it out." After pausing momentarily, he then menacingly asked, "Do I need to have you arrested and replaced?"

"No... it's ..." Nelson stuttered back nervously, "it's how we're doing it. Electrocution is so barbaric."

Completely engulfed in rage—and somewhat perplexed, Nelson's supervisor screamed, "Have you gone mad? They're robots... It's the only way to stop the virus from spreading."

The Tally of Victory
Sam M. Phillips

When the maxim guns lie silent and smoking, when the barrels of the repeating rifles are hot and their butts rest in the sand, grasped by tired white hands, the British officers go out to perform their morbid task. As the sun goes down and the sand of the desert cools, they walk amongst the Sudanese, many dead, most still dying. Concentrating, the officers count the fallen foes, ignoring their pitiful pleas for aid. Stepping over shattered limbs and spilt guts, they survey the battlefield, sigh silently, and then report back to their superiors the tally of victory.

Arild's Harvest
Roy C. Booth

For months Arild languished in his cell, a prisoner of King Erik of Sweden, a casualty of war. He and his family had lived peacefully for many years in Sweden, but when the war came, he was honour bound to serve in the Danish navy. Rescued after his ship sank, he became a prized prisoner, being a noble and all. But now he was truly miserable, for the letter in his hand from his beloved childhood sweetheart, Thale, told him that her father had chosen another man to be her husband, for he could not foresee Arild ever being set free, and the springtime marriage arrangements had already begun in earnest.

Feverishly, Arild wracked his brain all winter, trying to find a solution to both of his dilemmas. Finally, he requested to write a letter of his own, and to King Erik, he wrote:

Your Royal Majesty,

Once you called me a friend, and because of this I now ask you to grant me one favour: Allow me to return home and marry the woman I love and let me stay with her long enough to plant a crop and harvest it. You have my word I will return as your prisoner once I have completed the harvest.

FLASH FICTION ADDICTION

Arild's jailer took the letter and had it delivered.

King Erik's reply came swift and in agreement. That spring Arild emerged a free man—at least until autumn, harvest time.

Arild returned to his loving Thale, and her father allowed her to marry the man she loved. Arild then immediately went into the fields and planted his crop, as he had promised. He and Thale then prepared for harvest time.

When autumn came, Arild did not return to King Erik's prison. King Erik, puzzled since he knew Arild to be an honourable and sensible man, sent one of his housecarls out to fetch him. The herald rode off to Arild's farm and found the former prisoner in his field. Not a single plant was in sight.

"The harvest season is over; you must honour your agreement and return to the royal prison," said the housecarl.

Arild looked at him for a bit and then replied, "But I cannot harvest my crop." He gestured to the field. "Look, it hasn't even sprouted yet."

"Well, then, what did you plant?"

"Pine trees."

When the news of what Arild had done reached the king's ears, he declared, "A clever man like Arild should not be a prisoner! He is now and forevermore a free man!"

Arild and Thale lived together in happiness for many years, and today their forest still stands, a living testament to their love.

Finding Terence
Rich Rurshell

"My hair has gone!" cried Claude.

"So has your face, man," said Louis. Claude moved his hands from his scalp to the front of his head.

"So it has! How come you don't look so bad?"

"You died almost twenty years before me."

"I did?"

"Yeah, man. Too much partying."

"They were great times though, eh?"

"They sure were."

"How long have you been dead then?"

"No idea. I woke up today, just like you, like everybody else."

Louis and Claude watched others crawling out of their graves and leaving the cemetery.

"Jesus. Look at that poor bastard," said Louis, pointing to a torso pulling itself along the ground.

"Damn," replied Claude, still feeling at where his face used to be.

"I'm hungry. How about you?"

"I could eat."

"Let's follow that lot." They headed towards the cemetery gates, leaping over the torso as they went. They followed the shambling corpses towards the town centre.

"So, this is the *End of Days*," said Claude.

"Seems so," answered Louis. "It's not so bad, eh?"

"Can't complain."

"Better than being dead."

"I think we're still dead, Lou."

"Undead. I think that's the correct term."

"Hey! Whatever happened to Terence Gill? He'd know the correct term. He would love all this."

"As far as I know, that miserable bastard was still alive when I died. Yeah, he was obsessed by death. Listened to all that dirgy music."

"Let's find him," said Claude.

"How?" replied Louis.

"We should go to the register office in the town centre."

"How about after lunch?"

"Yeah. Good call."

* * *

"That was unexpected," said Claude, chewing on a severed forearm.

"Yeah!" replied Louis, biting off a piece of the large intestine he was carrying. "I'd never really thought of myself as a cannibal, but as soon as I saw those living folk, I got really hungry. Like, *really* hungry."

"Yeah. I don't know what came over me... Tastes pretty good though, eh?"

"Sure does."

When they arrived at the register office, the doors were locked. Claude looked at the opening times.

"Funny. It should be open."

"How do you know that?" asked Louis.

"The town hall clock said it was two o'clock."

"Maybe it's Sunday."

"Maybe."

"Anyway, I guess we are going to have to break in."

Claude nodded, and Louis stepped forward and put his foot through the lower pane of glass in the door. He kicked out most of the remaining glass and then crawled inside. Claude followed.

"Watch your face on those shards of glass, mate," said Louis.

"Screw you," replied Claude, giving Louis the finger.

"Shhh... what's that?"

Through the reception window, they heard sobbing.

"Hello?" called out Claude.

"Hello?" replied the receptionist. "Thank goodness, I thought when I heard..." She screamed as she saw Claude's skull staring back at her through the window and backed away.

"No, wait! We just want some information on our friend," said Claude. The receptionist stared at them for a moment, unsure.

"You won't eat me?"

"Eat you? No, we've just eaten. We're just looking for our friend, Terence Gill. We were wondering if you had a record of his death, or his place of burial."

"I can have a look. You'll have to give me some time though."

"Don't take too long," shouted Louis. "Claude here might rot away completely." Claude gave him the finger.

*   *   *

"Here it is!" said Louis, pointing at the tombstone. "Terence Gill, 1945 to 2018."

"Looks like he's still in there, let's dig him out." Claude and Louis started pulling away the soil from Terence's grave with their hands.

After a couple of hours, they finally got down to the oak lid of Terence's coffin.

"Let's crack her open," said Claude. They prised off the coffin lid.

"Terence!" shouted Louis. Nothing.

"Terence. Wake up!" shouted Claude. Again, nothing.

"Terence!" said Louis, giving Terence's shoulder a shake.

"WHAT?" screamed Terence as he sat up in his coffin.

"Terence... It's us. Louis and Claude," said Claude.

"I can see that. What do you want?"

"We're back, Tel. We're back from the dead. Everybody has woken up."

"I hadn't, had I?"

"Er... well, no..."

"Right. Well, fuck off then!" hissed Terence as he dropped back into his coffin, pulling the lid shut. Claude and Louis looked at one another.

"Sorry, Tel," they said in unison. There was no reply.

"Shall we put the dirt back in, Tel?" asked Claude. No answer. Louis shrugged and nodded his head. They began scraping the dirt back into Terence Gill's grave.

The Art of Team Building
Mel Lee Newmin

Recoil slammed the shotgun into Marilyn's shoulder. The impact jolted her and she nearly dropped the weapon. Only Quentin's quick reflexes saved it. Around her, five accountants howled.

Bill whistled.

"Not even close!" Jeremy hooted.

Marilyn glowered as her target, a clay pigeon, crashed unharmed onto the firing range.

With a gentle smile, Quentin helped Marilyn lift the gun to her shoulder again. "Give her a break, guys. She's never shot before." The thin, bespectacled man nodded encouragement. "Try again."

Marilyn's second shot knocked her backwards. Another clay pigeon sailed happily into the sunset while her co-workers scoffed at her inadequacies.

Disgusted by her boss's team building exercise, Marilyn handed off the gun and glared at Gavin's back as the vice president of finance sauntered towards the next firing station. Spending a day at the sportsman's club was his idea. Take the accounting department skeet shooting to develop camaraderie. Determine which of his boys has balls. Gavin hadn't considered the feelings of his one and only female employee on this, or any other day.

Marilyn despised him.

The shotgun rotated through the group. With each round, the men improved but Marilyn didn't. Her anger grew as one clay pigeon after another escaped death at her hands. While she waited between attempts, she pretended to enjoy the ridiculous affair. Her eyes, however, frequently strayed to the second station where Gavin and his three favourite accountants blasted away and cemented the already rigid departmental pecking order.

"Why do I feel like we're peasants and they're lords?" Bill mused, eyeing the second group.

"Because we are," grunted Jeremy before taking his next shot. "How stupid can a guy be? Giving guns to a bunch of subordinates who hate him? Clueless bastard."

Quentin's grey eyes glimmered as he watched his boss laugh it up with the chosen few. "He's lucky we suck at this."

Jeremy's hands clenched. "I'm not getting a bonus this year because of him. Gave me an unsatisfactory rating again this year."

"He does that to everyone so he hits his budget and earns his bonus," Quentin explained. He loaded another two shells into the gun for Marilyn, closed the breech and handed it to her. "Your turn."

Rather than take her shot, Marilyn instead raged when a wave of laughter erupted from the elite group. Because the stations stood only ten yards apart, she could see Gavin with his hands on his hips, his broad back in its crisp white shirt presenting a tempting target. If only someone on the accounting team knew how to shoot.

The team building exercise devolved into a gripe session amongst Marilyn's compatriots, each trading stories about how Gavin had screwed them over for vacation days or made them work evenings and weekends. Bill recounted when Gavin chewed him out for attending his own father's funeral on a day Gavin needed him.

The discussion grew rowdy. Bill pretended Jeremy was Gavin and playfully punched him. The two bumbled into Marilyn who held the shotgun. They bumped her arm. Her finger jerked on the trigger. The gun fired.

With a squeal, Marilyn dropped it.

The four accountants winced when the elite group hit the dirt.

"Oops," laughed Bill.

"Oh shit!" Jeremy pointed at the pandemonium in the second station. While the others had risen, Gavin was down.

In a panic, the four raced to help. Accounting Manager Peter knelt beside Gavin, pressing bloody hands into the VP's back to stem the bleeding. Marilyn's random shot had hit him square between the shoulders.

An ambulance was called, too late, and then the police. Because Gavin was dead.

Over the next three hours, detectives questioned the accountants. Everyone told the same story, that novice Marilyn had mistakenly shot her boss when she was bumped. Finally, after the incident was ruled an accident, the four accountants were released from questioning.

In sombre silence, Quentin trudged to his car carrying one of the guns he'd personally brought to the range. Marilyn followed with a second gun.

"You gonna be okay?" Quentin asked, popping his trunk.

Marilyn nodded. "Yeah, I think so."

Before Quentin could take the gun from her, Marilyn broke it and deftly caught the unused shells as they ejected. Then with a flick of her wrist, she snapped the gun shut and handed it to him stock first.

Quentin's mouth sagged open.

Marilyn winked. "You're welcome."

Taking the gun, Quentin didn't say a word.

Seth's Talks
A. L. Paradiso

Seven years and eight months after Impression, Seth and Ardee are sitting side by side on a gently sloping, grassy hillside which overlooks a bubbling stream. As they partake in their daily lunch, Seth pauses between sucking down barely-chewed chunks of meat to air his deepest thoughts, again.

"But, Ardee, we're bonded for life, committed deeper, stronger than all other bonds. Why aren't we more alike? Why can't we do the same things? I know your every thought, your every desire, sometimes even before you do. Why..."

"I hear you and I understand, Seth. I, too, often think how wondrous it would be if we each could do all the other does. But we can't, no matter how much we want it or you believe it. For example, you love music, but you can't write it, sing it or play any instruments. I can do all that."

"Yet we read each other's minds. I don't understand why I'm not as good or skilled as you are."

"It may be very true that we don't have the same skills, but you are much better than I in so many other ways. From the instant of our bonding Impression, you knew we were different. You needed me to feed you vast quantities of meat from the moment of your hatching, but you soon discovered your wings and how to hunt and how to feed yourself. You refused to see our differences from our first connection. *You* can fly and carry me high and far instantly. *You* can breathe fire. *You* can bespeak all other dragons and most people telepathically. I can't. Though you may not be human, you are a mighty, powerful dragon. We need each other, but not *to be* each other. Understand?"

A tiny, residual flame escaped him. "Ohhh, I suppose." Seth huffed, not totally convinced.

Lost Dog
Brian MacGowan

"I've lost my dog." A woman's voice cut through my concentration.

I didn't even bother to look up from my desk. "I don't do animals." I heard my door close. I rolled my eyes while I shook my head. Business may be slow, but not slow enough to look for a dog.

A damp umbrella slammed lengthwise across my desk, I jumped back. "I said, I lost my dog."

I glared at the umbrella, trying to get my temper under check. "And I said that..." I stopped myself when I gazed upon a gorgeous pair of... I looked higher... eyes. They were occupying a very pretty face surround by, hmm, blue hair with streaks of magenta.

I gestured to my guest chair. "I don't normally do animals, Miss?"

She leaned across my desk. "You will call me Mistress Elza. I did not lose an animal, I lost my dog. His human name is Mark Nessle, but answers to Princess."

I confidently sat back in my chair. "I see. Can you describe Princess?"

Mistress Elza glared at me. I idly brushed invisible crumbs from the desk. She sat in one of my chairs, pulling a Sharon Stone as she crossed her legs in front of me.

"Princess was wearing leather shorts with a shock collar. He is still a puppy in training so he has knee pads." She said this last bit with a sneer of disgust.

I wrote notes as I repeated her description. "Leather shorts, knee pads, shock collar around his neck."

"No! The collar was not around his neck, it was around his..." she smiled at me.

I tried not to be noticeable as I shifted uncomfortably in my chair. "Do you have an address for Princess? Perhaps he just went home."

"He is normally a well behaved puppy. He knows better than to leave without my permission."

I opened a browser on my laptop. "When did you first notice Princess missing?" I entered 'Mark Nessle' as the search term.

"I never see any of my dogs enter as humans. There is a discrete entrance that they use, from there they go to the transformation room, prepare themselves and wait for me in their kennel." Mistress Elza's veneer was starting to break. "This afternoon Princess was not in his kennel." She hesitated. "I waited, but Princess never showed up."

I looked at the search results, Mark Nessle was the CEO of a well known Wall Street company. I smirked to myself. "And did you go to the police?"

Mistress Elza stood up, grabbing the edges of her overcoat. She flashed me a cleavage enhancing red and black leather corset. "You have, no doubt, already searched up Princess' human name. For someone in his position, do you think this is an appropriate outfit to wear to the police station?"

I was certainly admiring the view. I looked back at the screen while trying to settle down my own, uhm, inner dog. A headline search caught my eye. "CEO killed in highway accident." Clicking on the link I quickly scanned the article.

I looked up at Mistress Elza. I spun the laptop around. She read the article, raising a hand to her mouth. "Foolish puppy," she sniffed.

Recomposing herself she reached into a pocket. "I apologise for taking up so much of your time." She pulled out a business card, placing it on my desk. "You may send your bill to this address."

She turned to leave. "Will you be okay?" I called out to her. She paused at the door, "Do you need someone to walk you home?"

Without turning she pointed to the floor behind her. "Heel!"

I stood my ground.

She turned to me. "Yes, please."

Outside, I offered her my arm. She hesitated before hooking her arm around. "Don't expect this all of the time," she said.

"Yes, Mistress."

Zero Days
Blake Jessop

"Do you remember me?"

Khalida narrows her eyes for a moment, then her face clears.

"Of course, I love you."

"Okay," I say, "do you remember you?"

* * *

The bay stretches below us. Morning fog rolls under the Golden Gate Bridge and makes it look like the masts of a ship lost at sea. Gulls wheel and cry.

"This is a wonderful," Khalida says.

"I wrote it for you."

"I take it I'm dead?"

She knows. What's the point of any of this if she already knows?

"You were wearing a cortical broadcast rig. I stole your engrams."

"I don't remember dying, how bad was it?"

"I don't know. You died, not me."

"Not the question," she says.

"You went on your terms."

"Then that's fine. I must have told you that would be fine."

"You did."

She looks at out the artificial San Francisco skyline. Light glimmers on the water like molten gold.

"Then what are you looking so sad about?"

"We never had a chance to say goodbye."

"Is that all?"

She wraps her arms around me and raises her mouth to mine. The kiss is as sweet and familiar as sherry on my lips.

"You know I hate long goodbyes, but I'm glad you brought me here. This is beautiful."

I can't help but smile. She always lifts me, always knows what to say.

"I thought we'd make a day of it. Go for a run, have a picnic."

"Then I bet I can beat you to the bridge," she says.

* * *

We run. This used to be a habit; every Sunday we'd jog from Fort Mason to the bridge, slap the concrete for luck, and turn for home.

The digital city is quiet. Noiseless but for the lap of wind and waves. No smog. No rules to bind us or lives to slow us down.

FLASH FICTION ADDICTION

We run, and when she pushes me to speed up, I accelerate faster than any human can.

"Not fair!" she yells after me, and I watch joy blossom as she learns to break the rules. We sprint and leap like superhumans through the city she loved.

*   *   *

We stop, eventually, out of breath. In a virtual reality you can run without tiring the same way you breathe underwater in a dream. I still pant. It's a thing human minds do. Khalida is sheened in sweat, amber skin flushed and radiant.

We picnic in the geometric shadow of the bridge, perspiration drying in a perfect breeze.

"This isn't so bad, as goodbyes go," she says.

"Is there anything else you want to remember?" I ask.

"One thing," she says, and slides a long, cool hand around my neck.

*   *   *

Khalida sighs and arches her back.

"This was a great day, but I'm done."

She has said that before, and it hurts as much as it ever did.

"I can't let you go."

"Yes," Khalida whispers, "you can."

She always says this, and she always smiles. No matter how I set the parameters. Always. I can't let her go, and I can't make her stay.

"I can't."

This is where I turn the simulation off. I've only let it go past this point once, because she asked me—

"Wait, how many times have we done this?" she asks again.

I bring up the menu. She swipes it out of reach.

"How many times have I asked you that?"

She looks at me and finds an answer. Tears flow from her eyes, full of life and rage and love.

"Goddamn it, swear. If you love me, erase me." She locks her peregrine eyes on mine. "Swear."

"I swear."

"Then, goodbye," Khalida says, and caresses my cheek and the kill switch at the same time.

*　　*　　*

Dragging myself out of the hormone rush feels like waking from death. I yank the Lacuna's radial ceramic mesh off my face and sit up gasping. The tablet by the bed reels off stats while cold rain uncoils against the windows. Night has come to San Francisco.

The screen gives me the iteration number and a count of how long I was under. *ZERO DAYS since last reset.* I get up and drink. The water tastes like rust. At the very bottom of the readout is her file name with buttons next to it, *LAUNCH* and *DELETE*. I hold Khalida in my hands, and try to hear her voice over the rain.

The Visitor
Michelle Perry

I sit by the window, wondering when my husband will visit. I hate this hospital, and the nurses with their little cups of pills. I can't think when I take them, so I hide them inside my cheek, then dispose of them. The day nurse, Patty, is apathetic, so it's hardly a challenge. Lisa, the weekend nurse, is more problematic.

It's been weeks since I hurt myself, so I wish they'd release me. I'm thirty five, too young to spend my life in a drug induced haze. I need to be home with Reed. I hope he still needs me, too.

When he last visited, I smelled perfume on his shirt. His affairs were nothing new, but they were usually fleeting, so I said nothing.

Suddenly, I see him on the sidewalk.

He's with Lisa.

Shock twists my stomach as she kisses him. He playfully swats her behind as she walks away, then smiles and twirls his keys on his finger.

He looks happy.

He enters my room a few minutes later.

"How are you today?"

I can't speak. He lays his keys on the sink and washes his hands. His wedding band is absent.

FLASH FICTION ADDICTION

I think of Lisa in my home. In my bed.

I seize his keys from the sink and stab him.

"Mum!" he croaks, clutching his spurting neck.

When he falls, I glimpse my stunned, sixty year old face in the mirror and realise he is not Reed, but the son I bore Reed.

"Caleb!" I scream. "Someone help!"

854814

Stuart West

Franklin stood in the gloom beside the other *dregs*, all three standing thigh deep in thick, acrid fluid far beneath the streets of the city. His faded blue jumpsuit was saturated with the foul smelling liquid and he shivered as he again dipped the net at the end of his long pole into the water. *Splish splosh. Splish splosh.* His once stocky frame had become lithe and his face gaunt. The lack of nutrients was surely the cause of his sallow complexion and the thinning of his greying hair but he had long ago ceased to care about his appearance. A wet cough from the broken individual to his right caused him to ponderously turn his head in the direction of the elderly creature whom shared his detail this week. He wore a jumpsuit bearing the number 854814.

Most sub-citizens, or dregs, lived beyond the boundaries of settlements. They avoided the fertile plains where the Labour Crews toiled to gather the crops to meet the demands of the city dwellers, living instead in the lawless uplands or the untamed wild lands. Some hid in the darkest parts of the cities, sustaining themselves on street vermin and the cast-offs of the societal elite. Following conviction for theft or trespass, the unlucky ones were forced to undertake the most undesirable tasks or face reprocessing as fuel or fodder.

FLASH FICTION ADDICTION

A half memory suddenly surfaced, almost causing a change in Franklin's unfaltering, vacant expression. 854814. That number—so familiar... Yes. It had been worn by the buoyant and energetic youth from Franklin's first shift. The boy had entered the chambers with a light heart and naive optimism gained living his life in the wilderness. He had faltered before long, of course. That said, it had been an accident that had finished him and not the slow wasting that took so many. Franklin remembered the look of terror as the boy had been taken by the current into one of the filters, the screams muted by the heavy water. He had tried to free the boy but it was impossible. He had strained and fought, yelling for help that would never come.

It was hard to gauge exactly how long he had been down here. With irregular shifts and a complete lack of sunlight it was impossible to know one day from the next. He pulled the net from the fluid once more, filled with matted hair and faeces. Without a thought, he flicked the foetid contents into the large plastic drum, balanced on the dry concrete ledge by the entrance to the chamber, and returned the net once more to the pool. *Splish splosh. Splish splosh.*

Franklin was the name given to him by his parents. He hadn't been born in the wildlands or raised in the alleyways out of sight, but had once held a position of standing in the city above. He had been a 'corporate' like his parents before him. He had worked to the best of his abilities for the betterment of the community in a towering edifice of glass and luxury. Another hacking cough from 854814 was followed by a string of incoherent murmuring punctuated by deep retching sounds that almost made Franklin wince. He glanced once more at his elderly companion as he deposited excrement, slime and a dead rat into the drum with a flop. This horrendous fool was using his sodden sleeve to wipe blood from his nose and chin; the rancid waters flowing freely from his mouth and eyes. Franklin almost managed to shake his head in disgust. There was no wonder they didn't last long— neither education nor common sense. The Dregs were closer to animals than people.

It was still unclear why he was here. A mistake perhaps? Regardless, the societal model that the Leader had forged for his great nation and the wider world was proven to be infallible. There would be a time when matters were set straight and when he could return to his rightful place in the Administratum—surely. There was a deep splash as 854814 slumped forward into the water and began to float slowly between Franklin and the outlet. With a grunt, Franklin pushed the floating man with his titanium-rimmed net toward the side of the chamber so he could continue with his work. The number was clearly visible on the back of the bobbing corpse. Franklin wondered for a moment if the suit would be a better fit for its next bearer before he dipped the net beneath the surface once more. *Splish splosh. Splish splosh.*

Gums
Daniel Craig Roche

When I was a drunk, I kept to myself, often drinking alone while watching the world move around me. It was peaceful back then, because people avoided me. But now that I've sobered up, I've become a part of that ever-moving world, and I've hated my life ever since.

There's a liquor store down the street from my work. I go inside every day and buy two nips on my way home. They're not for me, though.

There's this guy I call Gums. He hasn't got a single tooth in his mouth, and he sits on his big sheet of cardboard without saying a word. The skin surrounding his eyes could be tanned, or it could be filth. It's tough to tell. Either way, it's reminds me of leather. I adore this man because he's got the world by the balls. Always a half smile on his face, even when it's raining. People run past him, avoiding the puddles in the sidewalks. They have their pocketbooks and briefcases over their heads, protecting themselves from the rain as they hurry off to their meaningless existences. Not Gums. He just sits there with his half smiling face aimed straight at the sky. I've watched him. He hums to himself, enjoying each individual drop as it lands on his closed eye lids.

Gums is so cool. He doesn't even bother rattling his change cup, and when someone does drop something inside, he never mutters the words, *thank you*, and he never condemns people by saying, *God bless you.* He just sits and watches, the way I used to.

On my way into work this morning, I saw him sitting in his usual spot. Some people passed him while chatting on their phones, and some passed him while sipping their morning coffee. No one looked his way, however. Not even the ones who threw change at him.

He's watching though. Through those dazed eyes of his, he sees all.

His mouth cracks into a yellow grin the second my shadow blocks his view of the sun. We've never spoken before, and I intend to keep it that way. Our bond is too special for words. I hand him one of the two nips I bought, and he accepts it without praise. No *thank you,* no condemning *God bless you.* Just a nod of the head while he twists the cap free, then he downs the small bottle in one long gulp,

It's a beautiful thing to witness. I swear, my own belly grows warmer just watching it.

How wonderful it would be to crawl back into the bottle and return to those bittersweet days of an alcoholic daze. I might be sitting next to Gums right now. Happy. In the moment.

But I have to go to work. There's a box waiting for me, with a seat, a computer, and a phone. There's people living inside that computer, and living inside that phone, as well. People just like

FLASH FICTION ADDICTION

me, who are all a part of this ever-moving world, putting grease on its gears, oiling up that machine.

There's another nip in my pocket, though. If I were smart, I'd drink it, but I probably won't. Instead I'll give it to Gums, that peaceful man waiting on his sheet of cardboard, watching the world move around him. And as I watch him drink it, I'll remember the way it used to be. Back when I was like him.

Back when I was happy.

More Haste, Less Speed
L. T. Waterson

"Fuck."

Carl came out of the entrance to the tube station at a run. He was extraordinarily late.

"Fuck." He glanced at his wrist, the strip of paler skin attested to the fact that usually he wore a watch. In his mind's eye he could see it, lying next to the fucking useless alarm clock that had completely failed to wake him up this morning.

"Never a bloody clock around when you need one," he muttered to himself, ignoring the approaching couple who veered abruptly away when they noticed him.

He had not had time for a shower, a shave or even any fucking breakfast. His stomach rumbled on cue and the man's scowl deepened. To add insult to injury he was wearing last night's clothes. His cleaner, normally so reliable, had been off sick for a week and she was the one who normally took everything to the dry cleaners for him.

"Fuck, fuck, fuck." He tugged his phone from his trouser pocket and tried to focus on the screen. Four blinking digits should have told him what the time was but instead they blurred before his eyes and he swore again, "fuck."

FLASH FICTION ADDICTION

"Thanks mate." The words came from a rider, mounted pillion on a speeding motorbike. The bastard had just plucked the phone from his hand. "Like taking sweets from a baby." The mocking tone drifted back to his ears and he growled loudly.

For a moment Carl stood, staring nonplussed at his empty hand. Then he scowled. He should probably report the theft to the police, except how exactly was he supposed to do that when he no longer had a phone to call them with?

"Fuck!" This time the imprecation was shouted. He practically hurled the word at the uncaring people who were hurrying about their own business. He might as well have been invisible for all the notice they took of him.

"Fuck!" he shouted again. He saw a couple of heads actually twitch in his direction but still no one looked at him directly. London commuters are too well trained to ever make eye contact with a stranger, maybe he should test the theory out.

Carl shouted a few more times. He even executed a strange little dance and still nobody looked at him. Then he remembered that he was late.

"Fuck." That one was heartfelt as he was still a good twenty minutes away from his destination. This was it; he was going to have to run if he was to have any chance at all. Briefly he looked around but he was still being ignored. Good. Carl ran.

* * *

Twenty minutes later in one of London's big hospitals a group of anxious-faced nurses, a junior doctor, and a medical student gathered around a patient's bed. One of the nurses looked as though she was about to speak but the junior doctor looked at his watch, forestalling her.

"Time of death, ten thirty six."

The sombre atmosphere was broken as Carl raced into the room. All of those present turned to look at him.

Gasping for breath Carl screeched to a halt and said, "You wouldn't believe the shitty morning I've just had."

The Rabbits
Clement Wilson III

Ben will always remember the rabbits.

They'd been staying at his cousin Philip's farm. A year older and rather superior in his country upbringing, Philip considered Ben the poor city cousin.

After dinner, Uncle Robert and Milo, Ben's father, took the boys rabbiting, all rugged up with jackets, scarfs and beanies.

The men climbed into the ute, the boys clambered onto the tray with the lab, Chloe. Eight years old, she was a dab hand at rabbiting. At nine, this was Ben's first time.

The boys stood against the back of the cab, holding the rollbar as the ute traversed the rough terrain. To the first gate, the boys laughed so hard they were almost crying. But when the ute hit a hole, Ben's legs flew up, barking his knee against the cage.

The men were oblivious in air-conditioned comfort, so the boys wedged their elbows in the crooks of their knees. Chloe was having no difficulty staying upright, her tongue flapping in excitement. Four feet was an advantage.

Uncle Robert hit the brake, face planting the boys into the window. Even Chloe lost her footing.

The men got out, .22s in hand.

"You're on the spotty, Ben. Phil and Chloe are on pick up," Robert directed.

Milo set some ground rules. "Shoot forwards off the top of the ute, one gun at a time. Stay on the ute 'til you're told to get off."

Ben's heart was racing. He'd never seen a real gun. He stood, commanding the spotlight, and when he saw movement he turned the handle.

Bang! The rabbit froze in the cone of light.

"Good work," Uncle Robert said, raising his gun to his shoulder, peeling off a single shot.

The rabbit jumped, landing legs sprawled. As the shot sounded, Chloe was off, bounding over the landscape.

Is Chloe quicker than a bullet? Ben thought, because she seemed to arrive as the rabbit backflipped.

She held the rabbit limp in her soft mouth and high stepped over the tall grass.

Uncle Robert threw the body into the cage. "Who's up?"

Hands up, both boys burst, "Meeee!"

"Righto, Ben. Phil, you're on the spot."

Philip swept the spotlight back and forth. He saw the glint of eyes, swung it back and trapped the rabbit in the beam.

Uncle Robert stood behind Ben, holding the gun, positioning Ben's left hand under the barrel, his right hand over the butt, onto the trigger.

"Righto, breathe in, hold your breath, gently squeeze. Take your time, he won't move."

Ben heard his own heart. *Thud, thud. Thud, thud.* He took one breath, squeezed and Chloe took off.

Ben looked at Uncle Robert, "Where's Chloe?"

"You haven't killed it, mate. She won't retrieve if it's not dead."

Ben followed the men solemnly. The spotlight cast long, Drysdale figures on the canvas.

Chloe sat, proudly erect. Next to her, the rabbit twitched.

Uncle Robert crouched. "Good dog." He scratched Chloe behind the ears. Reaching over, he drew Ben in. "You've hit its hindquarters."

Ben steeled himself. The rabbit's leg and stomach had burst.

"Shall I get the gun?"

"Nah, mate. Bullets're expensive. Put it out of its misery."

Ben didn't understand. Did he mean a stick, a rock, what?

"Put your boot on its head, grab hold of its legs and pull til you feel its neck snap."

Fear coursed through Ben's veins. "Couldn't I just shoot it? I'll pay for the bullet," he begged. Philip sniggered.

"Nah son, take responsibility. Get it over with."

Ben leant down gingerly, held the warm, bloody legs of the rabbit. The rabbit saw its executioner. Ben stomped his boot down to hide its accusation, feeling its bulbous head and pulled with all his might, almost ripping one of the rabbit's legs off. The neck broke, a deadbolt sliding home.

Chloe grabbed the rabbit and bounded back to the ute.

Ben started to cry, dry retching. Adrenalin overflowed, leaving a sweet, metallic taste at the side of his tongue. He swallowed the bile, then swallowed again.

"It's okay, mate. You did good," Milo grabbed him, held him against his heart, the strong, certain beat reassuring him.

Uncle Robert was already halfway to the ute, talking to the night air. "You're up, Phil."

FLASH FICTION ADDICTION

Frank the Tank
M W Brown

The moment George stepped into the stuffy interview room he knew it was *the* Paul Carmichael sitting in the chair. Although he could only see the auditioner's back, he recognised the lopsided slope of his former class mate's broad shoulders. He recognised the sleek neck and square head of Stanton Manor's former head boy. Hell, he even had the same perfect hairstyle.

Despite being the UK's top film director, his last film grossed over 30 million in the British box office alone, George Sloan felt sick to his stomach. Nervousness prickled over his skin and drew out streams of sweat from his armpits.

George gulped, pulled himself up straight, and settled in between Laura, the casting director and Speccy, the producer. The stench of salty sweat and overpowering perfume did nothing for his nausea.

He slowly lifted his eyes from Paul's resume and stared straight at the middle-aged bit-part actor. Familiar dark, brown eyes eagerly looked back but they were set in a face that had wrinkled and plumped with age. The handsome teenager had turned into a tired, desperate man.

George pursed his lips as he stared at Paul. There was no flicker of recognition in Paul's eyes. George had changed his name, but after all the times Paul had shoved his face right up into George's, surely there would be some tiny spark of a memory?

Come on, Paul—don't you remember Frank?

It had been years since George had been called Frank and just thinking that name made George shiver. Frank Orlick was George's original name but after school was done, he couldn't shake the expected taunts anytime anyone said his name.

Some fucking recognition would be nice. Come on look at me. Really look at me!

George wanted him to know that the child Paul had tormented for six years was the now great George Sloan. A hot rage bubbled up through his intestines and hit the sinking disappointment causing a turbulent storm of frustration.

Paul's lips pulled back into a vicious snarl, and he stood up. George dropped his pen in surprise at the sudden movement.

"How're you doing Frankie-boy? How's Frank the Tank?" Paul stepped up to the desk and leaned over. "Have you licked any whores yet, Orlick? I bet you haven't. Just because you're some shitty director doesn't mean you get laid. I bet you're still a virgin."

Paul threw his head back and laughed. The smell of gum and stale cigarettes engulfed George, turning his stomach. The room felt as hot and stifling as the air in a crammed London underground train in the middle of a heatwave. He threw his hand over his mouth, clenching his trembling lips tightly together.

FLASH FICTION ADDICTION

"What's the matter, Whore Lick? Do you want me to stuff your head down the loo again, Whore Lick?" Paul slammed a cricket bat onto the desk. "Does Frank the Tank need a beating? We'll let you in our gang if you beg for a beating. Come on, Frank the Tank! Beg!"

George sprang back, sending his chair flying. "Get away!"

His looked wildly around. Laura and Speccy gaped at George, both with identical puzzled looks. Paul fidgeted nervously in his seat.

Laura rescued George's chair and rested her hand gently on his arm. "Are you okay?"

"Erm... yes. A fly... wasp... something... buzzy. All good." George sat down and tried to disguise his trembling hands by straightening the one-piece resume.

No! I refuse to be Frank the Tank again! Two decades of repressed anger and humiliation suddenly focused his mind.

"Laura's shown me your audition tape, but I don't think you will be suitable for the role of Tom." George tapped his pen on the desk and paused to fully absorb Paul's disappointment. "But..."

Hopeful eyes glistened at George. He revelled in the waves of Paul's desperation hitting him like a Tsunami.

"I'm thinking of having a new character written in. It's a bit of a challenging role—very physical. It's only a small part, but key. You'd be perfect."

Paul leaned forward in his chair, nodding vigorously. "Yes. Of course. Thank you. Anything—I'll do anything. I just need a break, a chance. I beg you..."

George rested his chin on his interlocked fingers. "The character is called Frank the Tank."

Boom! There it is. The flicker of recognition.

George put his arms behind his head and grinned.

We Named Her Olive
Alanah Andrews

We named her Olive, after the small copse of trees that we found her hiding in. A strong, proud creature—nevertheless, a single tranquilliser dart had been all it took to bring her down.

I gaze at her now, her slim form twitching with exhaustion on the cold concrete floor.

When she was first captured, we were elated; we finally had a breeding pair! But the excitement soon turned to disappointment, for our scientists never could produce live young that survived longer than a few days. They blamed Olive—she wasn't a good mother, they said—but I was never so sure. Perhaps some species simply reach their time limit on earth. Perhaps it just wasn't meant to be.

Her eyes are listless, almost transparent. A bowl of uneaten food sits in the corner of the small enclosure. My body aches with grief. Could we have done more to save their kind? Once, their population had numbered billions—and they had bred prolifically. That was unsustainable, of course, and we had labelled them as pests and slaughtered them for food and sport. But we had never meant to cull them into extinction.

By the time we realised what we had done, it was too late; a single breeding pair was all that was left. For thirty years we slowly lost hope that the breeding program might work. Three weeks ago, that hope had vanished entirely when Olive's mate began throwing himself repeatedly against the bars of the enclosure. I saw it on the video surveillance, Olive shrieking with alarm as he slammed into those metal bars over and over and over.

We were too late to save him.

When I removed his limp body, Olive was curled in the corner of the room. Three weeks later that is where she still lies. I think she blames us for his death. My supervisor disagrees; animals aren't intelligent enough to feel such emotions.

I gaze at her in awe and sorrow. The last of her kind. Such a waste. For three weeks she has starved herself. She is ready to pass on. We have tried our best to keep her comfortable. But still, there is a sadness about her which is haunting.

I let myself into the enclosure and crouch down beside her. She finally meets my eyes and I see my grief for her kind mirrored back at me. She opens her mouth and lets out a pitiful whine. I touch one of her paws gently. It is cold and hairless.

Taking a long shuddering breath, Olive's body spasms and then lies still. I sit with my back against the cage and dab at my tears with all six of my tentacles.

I hope when she is put on display they arrange her features so she looks proudly out at her visitors, chin jutting out in bravery as it was when we found her in that olive copse—the last of the human species.

Falling
Belinda Brady

It happened so quickly. One minute he was on the roof, the next he'd fallen. It looked like he didn't even call out. I was in the gym across the road from his house, watching the whole scene unfold before me through a window.

"Oh my goodness, he's fallen!" I cry, jumping off my treadmill, which continues our workout without me.

I run through the gym and across the busy road towards his house. I make my way to the back of the house, where he should have landed, bracing myself for a gruesome sight, only to be met with an empty patch of grass. He's not there. Even the ladder he'd been using is gone.

What?

"Hello dear, you're right on time. You must be a little shaken up. Please, sit and allow me to explain. The others will be here soon," a kind voice appears out of nowhere.

I turn to see an elderly lady behind me. She has wispy grey hair that has been pulled into a bun, a warm wrinkled face and a smile to match.

"What's your name?" she asks, as she takes my arm and leads me to a table set up against the back fence. It's laden with goodies and next to it is a fully stocked bar.

"Oh, I'm terribly sorry," I apologise, "I've interrupted your party. It's just I thought I saw, I thought...."

"It's fine, I know what you saw," the lady interjects, "now, tell me your name and I'll tell you all about what you've just witnessed."

"Angie," I murmur, scanning the yard for a possible quick exit.

"Nice to meet you, Angie, my name is Gretel. Please take a seat," Gretel gestures to a chair next to her.

Unsure of what to do I sit, anxiety churning away at my insides.

"What you witnessed was my husband, Albert, falling from our roof. You didn't imagine that. He was fixing a loose tile, lost his footing and fell. Sadly he didn't survive. While he was alive, he was always setting me up with new friends," Gretel chuckles softly, "I was a bit of a recluse and found it hard to make friends, while Albert was the complete opposite and just had a way of drawing people in. Everyone who met him just adored him. He wanted the same for me. The year after he died, on his death anniversary, a stranger ran into my yard, hysterical. They'd seen a man fall from the roof. But what they'd just witnessed was Albert playing out his death again, trying to attract new friends for me."

"New friends? What do you mean?" I ask, my confusion growing.

"Albert picks friends for me. He does this yearly. They're special. They're open to the spirit world - even if they don't know it yet - and they will see him. He knows we'll get along. We all do in fact. We get together every anniversary to welcome any newcomers and this year it's you. I can already tell Albert has made a wonderful choice. I have a feeling I'm going to like you." Gretel gets up and heads over to the bar, while I sit, head down, taking in her words.

"Can I get you a drink?" she asks. I look up to answer and gasp.

She's not alone.

A smiling Albert is next to her, complete in his death outfit. He gives me a little wave. Suddenly, a feeling of relief and happiness wash over me. I know I'm meant to be here and these people mean me no harm. This is the start of something special.

"Sure," I smile, waving back at Albert.
I have a feeling I'm going to like her too.

The Flat Cap
Isabella Fox

Still dressed in his filthy work clothes and favourite flat cap pulled low over his eyes, Corey knew he shouldn't be sitting in the pub drowning his sorrows. He should be hurrying home to Merry, his beautiful wife of three years. However, he had just been retrenched from his job in the coal mine and he really couldn't face her yet. Corey was a good worker but the industry was on a downturn. Retrenches were inevitable and because Corey was last in he was first out. He sat there thinking of his foreman's last words, "If it was up to me Corey it would have been one of those lazy Henry boys, but company policy is company policy, sorry."

Merry would only hug him and say, "It's alright Corey, you'll get another job and I have money coming in from my sewing. As long as we have each other we'll be okay." He knew she was right but somehow he felt he was letting her down so he sat there wallowing in self pity and slowly drinking himself into a stupor.

"Go home, Corey!" The barman ordered as he handed Corey his flat cap, which had fallen on the floor, and pushed him out the door. "Shit, I'm so drunk, I can hardly stand up," Corey muttered as he stumbled down the road towards home, a cottage three miles out of town. Glancing at his watch he wished he hadn't stayed at the pub so long and drunk so much. Merry would be worried about him. "I'll cut through Farmer Brown' cow paddock. That'll save time." he said as he swayed and staggered along.

Halfway across the paddock Corey tripped and fell flat on his face. His flat cap flew off his head and landed somewhere in the long grass. Corey blindly felt around, found his cap and shoved it back on his head. He stood up and swayed on his feet for a few minutes before continuing home without further mishap.

There, standing at the cottage door, was Merry. She looked at him and burst out laughing.

"Oh Corey, I don't know why you've come home drunk but next time perhaps you shouldn't come through the cow paddock!" She ushered the confused Corey through the door and placed him in front of the hall mirror. There perched on his head, instead of his favourite flat cap, was a large dry cow pat. "Come on Corey, let's have supper and you can tell me why you are so drunk," she laughed. "We can find your flat cap tomorrow."

Harold's Last Day
Austin P Sheehan

As he drove the company's van through the darkness towards the city, Harold turned up the heating against the chilly morning air. It was mid September, but the mornings still weren't getting any warmer. He thought of his kids, safe and snug in their beds. Harley and Sophie didn't know what he did. Nor did Sara, his wife of ten years. He didn't know how to answer when she asked, and usually said something about sanitation and changed the subject.

"When you get right down to it, it's pest control," his colleague Cole often joked. Harold laughed whenever Cole said it, though it was only funny the first time. And today he wondered if he'd even found it funny then. Cole always cracked jokes, but was very competitive with their work. He'd always try to fill up his van and deliver the cargo first, giving updates over the radio.

"I'm half full, H-man. How 'bout you?" or "I got me some real stinkers today, Harry. They stink so bad I'm gonna need a whole new van!" Occasionally Harold rose to the challenge, tried to fill his van first and beat Cole making delivery, but those days were rare. Ultimately, Harold was reconsidering the contract. He knew few people loved their job, and that he was paid very well.

FLASH FICTION ADDICTION

And maybe he enjoyed it at the beginning, but not now. Not since one brutally cold morning about a month ago.

"When you get right down to it, it's pest control!" Cole yelled at him from the roof of his van, catching as much of the weak winter sun as he could. Cole was wrapped in a thick grey coat, wore a battered faux fur hat and a broad grin. He was yelling to be heard over the powerful pressure hoses blasting the van's steel interior, over the thumps and screams of the terrified cargo.

After parking the van and pulling on the brown leather gloves Sara had given him for Christmas, Harold looked up and down the street. No one in sight, just a bench lit by a streetlight, struggling to shine through the thick fog. As he approached the figure on the bench, he recalled that icy morning and Cole's happy face. Whispering 'pest control' to himself, Harold slipped a black plastic bag over the homeless woman's head. While stifling her cry and restraining her flailing arms, he was struck by an odd phrase; 'there but for the grace of God go I.' He carried on, thinking it must be from a movie he'd seen, or from the radio.

Harold dragged the sedated cargo to the van, threw her onto the steel bench bolted against the wall, and restrained her wrists and ankles. All the while trying to place where he'd heard that phrase before. It stuck with him as started the van and drove on through the dark city streets.

He soon found his next target. An old man was curled up under a tattered coat, sleeping on a cardboard mattress behind a grimy tattoo parlour. The fog had lifted, and Harold approached the dark shape, bathed in soft moonlight. He watched the grey hairs flapping across the withered face, listened to the animalistic snore emerging from the open mouth, and saw more gaps than yellow misshapen teeth. "There but for the grace of God go I," he whispered.

Breathing in, he looked up to see dark clouds approaching, heavy with rain. Harold considered the approaching downpour, the blasts of the pressure hoses, the thumps and screams, and his colleague's laughter. Breathing out, determination laced with fear tightened his stomach. Returning to the van, he opened the back, then uncuffed and slung the sedated woman over his shoulder. Without rousing them, he placed her next to the old man, and left them both shivering on the cardboard mattress.

"Cole, I'll be late getting back today. Over." Harold's gloved hand hung out the window, tapping a steady rhythm on the van's smooth exterior.

"Roger that," replied Cole. "Bet I kick your ass tomorrow too, Harry! Over and out." Harold glanced at his watch. It was still early. He couldn't take the van back empty. And he couldn't deliver the cargo they wanted. With grim resolve, Harold drove towards the banking district and courtrooms of the city, preparing to make his final delivery.

"When you get right down to it, it's pest control," he said, grinning to himself in the mirror.

The Grind
Marlon Hayes

My commute to work is the worst part of my day. I live south of the city and my job is west of the city, so I drive for an hour. Construction, rush hour, school buses, and people who should not be allowed to drive add to my misery.

I kissed my little boy Jarrod before I left. His kisses are sweet and wet, and he makes me smile. He's a typical little boy, loving to get dirty and play with his toys. My mother watches him while I'm at work, and she's under his thumb. Maybe it's the sweetness of his kisses. He knows his colours and his letters, and we're teaching him to read. I love reading to him, and Jarrod loves Dr Seuss and Goodnight Moon.

Traffic is crawling, and I resist using the horn. It wouldn't make a difference. It's rush hour and the only way to make it to work on time is to leave twenty-five minutes sooner. The radio station I listen to at this time of the day focuses on love and relationships. I listen despite how much I disagree with what's being said. There are women who are bitter towards men without acknowledging the part they played in the relationship. I sabotaged my relationship with Jarrod's father on my own, with no help from anyone else. Honesty and transparency are building blocks for a successful relationship, but those are not necessarily going to be accepted by the significant other. Some secrets aren't meant to be shared.

    I park in my spot when I get to my job. The security officer waves and I return it with a smile. Not a flirtatious smile, but a smile of recognition. I don't know whether he's attracted to me, but it doesn't matter. I will never date someone from my job, because it never works. I know there are people who date their co-workers but it only leaves bitterness and resentment which leads to one or both parties needing to find employment elsewhere. I am kosher when it comes to dating at the workplace; meat and cheese do not go together.

    Jarrod and I watch a lot of Disney stuff. We sing and dance to the different songs, and I want to take him to Disneyland. I'm pretty good at saving money, and I'm saving to buy a house for us. I'm cautious in my decision-making these days. As much as I want to take my son to see Mickey, I'm not willing to loot my savings for it. I'll find another way as usual.

    I settle in at my work station, change into my uniform and I'm dressed for my shift when my co-workers arrive, right before the shift starts. We exchange perfunctory greetings and that's all. I'm not friends with any of the people I work with. I've learned to keep business and my personal life separated.

    The problem with being so private is I don't let people into my life, which led to the breakup with Jarrod's father. He felt as if he should know everything about me. I felt as if certain things were on a "need to know" basis, so when I finally told him everything about me, it finished us. We get along fine as co-parents and he's moved on. I feel pangs of regret because we could have been good together.

I have a bachelor's degree and my friends who graduated with me are miserable in their chosen fields as teachers, social workers, etc. They complain about the kids, the hours, and their paychecks. They borrowed upwards of $100,000 and make less than $30,000. It's not fair or equitable, and my dreams require real money. I average about $2,000 a week, saving money each month for my house and some kind of business venture. I don't plan on working for someone else much longer.

I believe in me.

Recently I started dating again, and Mario is a nice guy, full of dreams and plans. It's been three months and things are progressing nicely. I'm not yet at the honesty and transparency stage. I'm inching along. After Disneyland, I'm going to ask Mario to travel to Jamaica with me. Maybe a getaway will be the thing that convinces me to open my heart to him. We'll see.

The bell sounds, prompting us to start our shift. As I perform my first lap dance, I keep repeating *Disneyland* over and over again, a new dangling carrot to get me through the night...

Serve Cold
David Bowmore

I develop recipes for TV chefs. I'm the one who decides if the ingredients work, tweak them a bit if necessary, a pinch of salt here or added flair there.

Anybody who thinks the Jamie's and Ramsey's of this world can do it all themselves is deluded. These guys are millionaire business people with restaurants, television programmes, and books to promote all around the world. They have charities to patron and families to be perfect with. They do magazine interviews, tweet their news, facebook their envious lives, and don't forget occasional TV spots. They give the impression of being superhuman, but they have large teams to support them in every aspect of their lives.

I currently work for a particular lady who's been in the biz for what feels like centuries. She has it all, the big house, a successful business, a football team, and a perfect family. All built on lies and deceit. Back in the day when we were just starting out, we both worked for Craddock as assistants. Her on screen and being helpful. Me behind the scenes, doing the sweaty work. When Fanny had had her day, someone new was needed to fill the void. She stole my creamed chicken recipe, and it wasn't the last thing she stole. After she dumped me, and I was dropped from the production, I saw many of my dishes served up with a tweak here or a pinch of salt there. However, through grit and determination I got other work behind the scenes and the chaps with the big names were always appreciative of the help of backroom boys like myself. I'm grateful, but damn it, I deserved the top gig. I should be the recent receiver of an OBE. I deserve everything she has instead of a flat I can barely afford the rent on and a tumour the size of a fist in my bowel.

A year ago I was asked to be part of her team. She didn't recognise me—bitch.

There she is now smiling at the camera, putting the almond tart in the oven. Listen to her: "Cook for twenty minutes on gas mark four or fan one eighty." Senile old cow got it wrong, again. "Then leave for an hour until cold."

Now they cut to my tart, and she simpers, "Fortunately, I made this one earlier."

She cuts a thin wedge and serves it with raspberries and crème fraîche. The camera lingers over my masterpiece. Then with a fork she cuts the tip off the slice and raises it to her pouting red lips. She slips the portion in, sucks the fork with sensual pleasure, licks her lips, and smiles at the camera. Her eyes still as alluring as ever, look beyond the camera into the homes and lives of everyone watching. The viewers at home can taste it.

"Astounding, nothing better. You'll love it."

I had loved her once.

Everything happened so quickly. Grasping her throat and foaming at the mouth she collapsed forward, crashing off the work counter and landing on her back. She was dead before she hit the floor, live on Saturday morning TV.

We all rushed forward to help, but I stopped at my almond tart and cut myself a slice.

I smiled as I took my final bite, and thought of the old adage about cold dishes and revenge.

Elsie
Jean Frost

Hello, my name's Elsie Stratford and I'm six years old. It was my birthday yesterday and also the day I started work. Yes, *six* years old—Mam kept me back an extra year because I'm so small. She said she wished she could send me to school like the boys but it's more important that boys can read and write and we need the money because wages have gone down and I'm eating more.

It's my job to sweep the floors to get back the metal. The more metal I find, the more I get paid. I got a whole penny yesterday but Mam says that's because the previous girl died and the floors hadn't been swept for days. She bought enough potatoes with my penny to last all eight of us for the week and the grocer gave her some carrots that had black spots for free. I felt so proud to be helping my family.

I need to get in the corners more, me being so small should help with that. Ethel says her baby brother is bigger 'n me. Mam says Ethel needs to keep her mouth shut.

I thought sweeping floors would be easy, I didn't know I'd be crawling under the thundering grinding-wheels while they were still spinning. The work is dusty and I already have a cough. Mam got me a sack from the foundry. It doesn't have too many holes and it's tied around me with a bit of old rope so I don't get my clothes too dirty. It trails right past my knees.

The women smile at me kindly but I don't understand what they say. I said one of the words at home last night and Da gave me what for. He says I must never talk like them, or the minister won't give us food. I don't like the minister, he makes me feel sick inside the way he looks at me.

I can't talk much longer; the foreman is glaring at me. Mam says he's all right unless I annoy him too much. Maggie is always smiling at him and brushing up against him. Rose says that if she keeps that up there'll be babbies. If that's how you get babbies, I'll run away the next time the minister does that to me.

Time to tuck my hair back in my bonnet. One of the older girls gave it to me—the last girl wouldn't wear it and her hair caught in the grinding-wheel.

That's how she died.

FLASH FICTION ADDICTION

The Woman in the Window
Arwen West

A figure of darkness and shadow, I do not know who she is or where she comes from. She appeared one day and never left. I remember my creaking footsteps falling silent in the crooked corridor of the top floor when I first saw her. She was sitting on the window seat, staring outside with those empty, reddened eyes. It was a frosty morning and the biting cold reached into the old wooden house and chilled my quick breaths, making tiny clouds in the air before me. She didn't turn. She didn't move. She just stared.

Sometimes when I am falling to sleep her shrieking makes my heart beat fast. I'm sure that people from miles around shiver at the sound of that echoing voice but nobody ever mentions the noises. When I took the others to see her, she wasn't there and they thought I was teasing. From the street where the smaller children play you can just see her silhouette. Always watching. Never moving.

My parents say I am being silly and Doctor Bob sometimes looks worried. I'm not sure if she is as real as the rest of the world, or just something my mind has made up like they whisper to each other, but every time I go to bed she comes to my dreams and I get scared. I think that when we first came to this house she was searching for someone and I fear she has chosen me. Sometimes I sneak up the stairs by myself and peak along that horrible corridor and she is always there. Waiting.

Hungering
Laurie Bis

"Check over there! I heard something rustling around in the underbrush," a deep voice called out in the darkness.

John squatted down in scant protection of a shrub at the top of a slight incline. He watched the two torches moving about where he'd just been a couple of moments earlier.

"Uhn uh," came the hushed reply. "No way am I going any closer to that forest. You want to, go right ahead—I'll send my condolences around to your wife"

"You superstitious little coward!" sneered the deep voice. "Fine you win—we'll come back in the morning with the dogs if they'll make you feel better."

"Caution isn't cowardice, Stewart. Those sheep weren't killed by a fox. There's blood on the moon and whatever slaughtered them was far more dangerous than anything we've come across so far. Don't tell me the hairs on the back of your neck aren't sticking up too. It's out there watching us."

From his hidden spot a glittering pair of green eyes watched as the two men, voices growing fainter as made their way back toward the farmstead that had lit up when the alarm was raised. Once he was sure they weren't coming back, he finally stood. The wind shifted in his direction, wafting the scent of slaughtered sheep to him. Hunger threatened to overtake him again. He managed to push the urge back, unconsciously wiping a trail of gore across his pants. He took one last hungry look at the farmhouse in the distance before retreating into the dark sanctuary of the forest.

From Urn to Oak
Lozzi Counsell

Tracey dusted the urn.

"Get some rest, Arthur. You have a long day ahead of you tomorrow." Arthur groaned—he was known as the grumpy old man of the retirement home and this had only gotten worse since his wife died.

Tracey lingered in the doorway for a while, looking back before turning the light off and shutting the door.

Arthur waited until he heard her steps lead down the far end of the hallway, before climbing quietly out of his bed and slipping his feet into his slippers. The nurses wanted to accompany him to have his wife's ashes scattered, but he wanted to do it alone. They had told him time and time again that he wasn't strong enough to do it alone and that he would never make the journey in his old state, but Arthur was 'goddamn stubborn' as Tracey would say. Luckily for him, his bedroom was on the ground floor.

He wrapped his dressing gown around him, tucked Bernie under one arm and pushed the window open, before stepping over the sill. He could already see his destination right in front of him.

He trailed the carpark, followed the meandering river through a farmer's field and finally stood defiantly at the bottom of the hill they'd both shared dreams about from the safety of their little bedroom, ever since being in the home.

"It's alright, love. We'll get there soon." Arthur puffed. He stroked the urn, before starting off up the hill. His eyes were fixed on the large, lone oak right at the top where they'd stared in wonder at the many wind chimes dangling from its hanging branches.

It took him a while to get up the muddy slope and he even lost a slipper on the way, but not even the squelch of mud between his toes could take away his happiness and relief when he finally crested the rise.

The tree was even more beautiful up close, especially as you could now hear the gentle chimes in the night's breeze.

"I told you we'd make it, Bernie. Sleep well, my love." He opened the lid of the urn and let Bernie's ashes blow away. But now he was tired. So tired. So he sat down against the trunk of the oak tree, laid the empty urn on the ground beside him and closed his eyes. He smiled. It seemed the nurses had been right after all. And as his heart gave way and he took his last breath, some of Bernie's ashes fluttered down and laid to rest on Arthur's still body.

Squids Aren't Monsters
Karen Thrower

Anatomist Richard Owen stared at the creature the crew of the HMS Daedalus had captured. It was clearly a squid, and no one would argue that fact except for the creature's enormous size! Squids are normally around a foot or two in length, but this one was at least forty feet long. It floated in a giant tank in the hold of the Daedalus, normally reserved for the fish they would catch. The lights this aquatic monster was giving off from its head lit the entire hold, rendering the need for a torch superfluous. It reminded Dr Owen of Morse Code, and he wondered if this giant could communicate with humans. He stepped up to the tank and tapped out 'hello'. But the flashes it responded with were gibberish.

Dr Owen scoffed and sat on a nearby box, pulling a small notebook and a pencil out of his jacket pocket. He knew he had to make notes on this monster before he forgot. 'This colossal monster the HMS Daedalus has put in its hold, is nothing more than a squid of considerable size. Currently, the reason for its colossal size is unknown. It could be the result of its diet, or even the cold water at depths that man dare not travel. The flashing I have observed from its mantle, may help it communicate with other squids. But after a quick test it was determined that it does not know Morse Code. As such, we are unable to communicate with this impressive monster.' Richard sighed and sat back, trying to crack his back when he noticed the squid's head was poking out of the tank, looking at him.

"I am not food for you." He said playfully, wiggling his finger at it.

The squid's head tilted to the side and he swore he heard a watery scoff. "As if I would stoop so low," a proper British accent replied.

Dr Owen's eyes went as wide as he dropped his notes and got to his feet. "Did... did you speak?" he managed to say.

"Of course, I did." Owen watched as one of its long tentacles stretched from the tank and picked up the notes he had dropped onto the floor. "What did you write about me?" It asked and quickly read the notes. It seemed to look between him and notes several times. "Sir, impressive or not, I am no monster!" It sounded offended as it threw the paper down on the floor. It heaved itself out of the tank and slapped two of its wet tentacles against Richard's chest. "Just because I am of considerable size, does not mean you can label me as such!" It made its way up the stairs to the upper deck. Dr Owen swore he heard the squid muttering angrily to itself as it moved. Its tentacles smashed through the door and the crew yelled in response. "Boorish creatures!" The squid yelled. Dr Owen heard a large splash and assumed the squid was gone. The captain of the Daedalus came running down to the hold, lantern in hand.

"Dr Owen! Are you all right?" He stopped by the tank and marvelled at how it was empty.

Richard cleared his throat and straightened his jacket. "Yes, Captain, I'm alright."

The captain turned and looked at him the best he could with the lantern. "Were you able to learn anything from it?"

He took a breath to steady himself. "I learned that, apparently, squids aren't monsters." He laid his hand on the captain's shoulder. "Let's, uh... let's not speak of this again."

Arthur's Tale
Colin D. Palmer

When I was four years old, I probably did what all four year old's did. I don't know because I remember nothing from when I was four.

Except the nightmares, and luckily I only remember them when I'm asleep.

Today, I don't even know if those nightmares were real. Time has a way of dealing with unpleasant thoughts, either blunting them with vagary or obliterating them altogether. I feel sorry for those that recollect everything with apparent clarity of perpetual detail. I'm glad it isn't me. That's a bit of an understatement—I'm absolutely ecstatic it isn't me. The vague and the non-existent is a far better proposition, thank you.

I'm positive I would have thrown myself from a very high place by now, if I retained memories of things I'd rather not have. Still, in the dark of night, lying in bed, or peering at the night sky out from the balcony window, sometimes I see, or hear things, little scratches, little moans, a flash of light, great shiny teeth from a maw the size of Jupiter, some jolting piece of nostalgia I've learnt to ignore.

The horror I have to relive every time I close my eyes and go wherever it is that sleep takes us, has a way of living inside me and everyone else that dreams the same way, I guess. Fortunately, waking up dissipates whatever went on under cover of darkness and closed eyes.

    I don't want to know.

    What I already know is that it's not good.

    Sleep is rare these days. I know that's because I have time on my hands now, but time has a way of helping one remember. Sleep and time in combination are an even better catalyst for inducing memories.

    Memories I'd rather not recall. Ever. If I can help it.

    Sleep, I can try to control. Time, however, is out of my hands.

    My eyes are closing right now, forcing the understanding that even some sleep is necessary. Sometimes. I don't want to. Sleep. I sit up straighter and stare out the window, the half crescent of a moon smiles back at me as the stars wink their existence, an exuberant display of cheekiness bordering on the suggestive.

    Go to sleep, they are saying.

    No way.

    Come on, it'll be fun.

    Thanks, but no thanks.

    Want to play a game?

    No. Go away.

    We want you, Artie.

    Everyone wants me. Leave me alone.

La Luna smiles at you, Artie.
Yes, I can see that.
With your eyes closed?
Yes. Yes. Too heavy. Eyes closed, head drooping. Moon laughing, stars winking, teeth sharpened, mouth extending.
Here we go again.
This time is different, though. This time, you're coming with me.
I hope you don't have a retentive memory or you may wake up like the last person who accompanied me. That sad event was about ten years ago and signalled my one and only adult relationship. I guess we got to share one night together. I carry exceedingly vivid and pleasant recollections of the occasion. Mostly. Time will get rid of them, but until then, I will fight to keep those memories as long as possible. We had a romantic photo taken at dinner, which I still have, and that helps too.
She woke up screaming. That piercing scream jolted me back and awake in an instant, to be met with thrashing arms, bared teeth, wild eyes and slashing nails as she backed up tightly against the bedroom wall, away from whatever it was terrifying her. At the time I could see what *it* was and understood and shared her desperate fear. Time fixed that. I have no idea what it was now. Her though, I still remember. And always will. Well as long as I can anyway.

FLASH FICTION ADDICTION

I can smell her perfume—which is strange, because that usually happens only when I'm asleep. Oh, that's right. I am asleep. You too.

See the moon smiling at you now? The moon is happy because I've brought someone else to play with. You ready?

Come on, it'll be fun.

Yes, we're waiting.

We can play games.

Close your eyes.

Let's go.

All in a Day's Work
Melanie Waghorne

The hospital corridors are dimly lit. Visiting hours have long since passed. The majority of rooms I pass are quiet except those whose occupants are heavily snoring or being kept alive by the seaside swooshing noise of a respirator. I glide along on tiptoes to stop the squeaking of my shoes alerting anyone to my presence. Carefully scanning the corridor I duck into an open room and push the door shut, hearing the soft snick of the lock coming home. The sound of my ragged breath and the steady rhythmic beat of a heart monitor are resonant in the room. I try to gather myself before I draw back the curtain. I don't think I'll be able to do it if his eyes are open. They are closed. I have no excuse.

I watch the fluttering of his chest, the painfully slow rise and fall as he sleeps, his breath as light as moth wings. I follow the dart of his eyes under paper-thin lids. I hope his dreams are sweet. I gaze over his emaciated body, know I am doing the right thing. The syringe in the front pocket of my tunic felt so obvious as I walked down the corridor, like a pubescent boy trying to cover up a hard-on in a public swimming pool. I draw it out now and hold it across a trembling palm. I've done my research, know that this will be the agent of salvation, whether his or mine I can't remember.

FLASH FICTION ADDICTION

The needle tip slips into the crook of his elbow easily, the translucence of his elderly skin showing a vein in stark relief. I pull a little blood back into the chamber, watch it bloom and dilate within the solution before plunging the mixture deep into his vein. I smooth the bubble of blood that blossoms as I remove the needle. I'll keep a little of him on the pad of my thumb, his life force staining the whorls and ridges there. Pulling the covers a little tighter around him I resist the urge to kiss his forehead, pleated and creased by the memories of a life well worn. The syringe trembles a little as I try to get it back into my pocket. I can see the scenario in bleak terror through my mind's eye, having to scrabble under the bed for the clear tube holding my fingerprints, my guilt stamped there. Thankfully my quivering fingers find purchase, delve it deep back into my pocket. I pull the curtain, like a shroud back around his bed.

I tumble into the corridor, as unstable as a newborn fawn. Already the hitch and struggle in his breathing is evident. The heart monitor begins to speed, matching the cadence of my own. I walk away from his room, try to seem confident—heel, toe, heel toe. Look ahead. The squeak of my soles makes me wince at every contact. The beep behind me has reached a crescendo, something unmanageable, on the brink of disaster. My throat tightens as the flat-line tone rings out. I have to stop myself running from it, the high pitched keening of a wounded animal, just behind me, stalking me down the linoleum corridor. Tears gather at the corners of my eyes.

An alarm sounds up ahead in the nurse's station, mimicking the one behind me. I am trapped between the two sounds, battered by them. I duck into another room as the crash team surge towards me, racing to save the life of the man who I have just... What? What is the word that will make me feel okay about what I have done? Mercied? Euthanized? Sent to a better place? Killed.

I hunker down on the other side of the door. Listen as they yell to each other about Atropine and paddles. My hands clasp my ears as the flat meaty sounds of the defibrillator making contact drift through the corridor. I try to slow my own heart, beating strong and hale in my chest. Concentrate on it—one, two, three. Breathe. Hot saliva squirts to the back of my mouth, I swallow noisily trying not to be sick. The door jamb is mercifully cool as I lean my flushed face against it. When the jitter in my limbs begins to subside I stand, smoothing the creases of my clothes, pushing the hair away from my burning face. Composure. I walk back out into the corridor.

"Good evening, Matron."

I smile and nod, walking slowly and calmly towards the nurses' station.

"Good evening," I reply.

A Lover's Dwelling
Randal Eldon Greene

Heart: Here, Lover, you may dwell. I am an open, womb-like space made ready.

Brain: Lover, thoughts of you have been constant, but no verdict has been reached. You may someday dwell here as a dream running in the unconscious background. Or dwell as a looping image at the forefront of the mind—a longing. Possibly even as a trauma, far in the future, if need be. But first these constant thoughts must find a resolution to the question of you: "To let the lover dwell or not to dwell."

Heart: Ache and openness are my natural states. Lover, you are welcome to come in. I am a house and your beauty is a key to my door.

Brain: I think of you, Heart. I see, Heart, how you invite without logic.

Heart: Brain, you make me ache. I want to speak in mazes; Brain, you wish to speak in solved equations.

Brain: Finishing a puzzle before declaring the picture is necessary to make an accurate judgement. Good judgement means a good life. A good life means using judgement to make a logical choice of lover.

Heart: Love is never a choice. Therefore you, Lover, may join with me. Bring your whole self. I wish to consume you.

Brain: Heart, hold up, can Lover provide comfort, care, constant companionship? Can Lover occlude, eclipse, make you, Heart, blind to all other beauties in the world?

Heart: Lover, I am flying. The doubts—they come from Brain, a stupid nag.

Brain: Heart, listen! Listen up! We do not want woe. We want the same thing. There is no rush.

Heart: I want Lover. Now.

Brain: We want happiness, Heart.

Heart: I want to make Lover happy. I sacrifice my will to Lover.

Brain: Are you really so selfless and selfish at the same time?

Heart: Lover is a paradox that unfolds into the sameself lover. Lover, unfold in me. Line the walls of my being with your presence. Join the beat of my palpitating longing.

Brain: Lover, let me interrogate you before Heart draws you irrevocably in. Let me ask first, decide about loving later.

Lover: Ask what?

Brain: What will you give me?

Lover: Love.

Brain: How will you give it to me?

Lover: Through my mouth, my crotch, my words, my soul.

Brain: What is the duration of this love?

FLASH FICTION ADDICTION

Lover: Forever and ever and ever.

Brain: How can I trust your love?

Lover: You know, I'm getting kind of bored of this Q&A.

Brain: Are you? Are you easily bored?

Lover: Uh, sure . . . Want to watch a movie or something?

Brain: Well, this is important. We should really finish this first.

Lover: [Yawn] I'm not really in the mood right now, you know.

Brain: Well, if not now, when? I want to come to a resolution—a decision. Let's just finish now. Come on.

Lover: Yeah, you're being kind of needy.

Brain: Me, needy? I'm being logical about this.

Lover: Logic is overrated. You've got to just roll with it once in a while.

Heart: I agree!

Brain: Roll? Listen, if we can't address these issues—talk about our love—what's the point of moving forward?

Lover: Speaking of rolling, I've got to roll.

Brain: Wait.

Lover: Bye.

Heart: No! Stop! —Brain, how could you overthink this?

Brain: How could Lover underthink this?

Heart: This is your fault. Once again, I am a broken, aching mess because of you.

Brain: It's obvious that I have saved us from the doldrums of an incompatible lover.

Heart: You have destroyed my future. *Our* future.

Brain: You're being dramatic.

Heart: You're being heartless—cold and logical.

Brain: You'll mend. No heartache lasts forever.

*　　*　　*

Lover: Hey. I'm bored. Want to hang?

Heart: Here, Lover, you may dwell.

Brain: Lover, thoughts of you have been constant.

Growing Flowers
James Pyles

Raise your words, not voice.
It is the rain that grows flowers, not thunder.

– Rumi

It wasn't Santiago's blindness that had caused him to neglect his gardening tools, because after all, he did not need to see in order to tend the heucheras and campanulas. It was the machine that took up all his time. He chuckled as he recalled the sculpture of the brass Buddha welded on the steel beam next to the fused length of chain, which he had purchased and placed in the humble garden before glaucoma stole his sight.

"Keep the balance, eh?" He adjusted one of the control cogs and then let out a length of cable from beneath what his family called 'the contraption.'

Having aged past seventy, he was still limber enough to sit cross-legged on the ground in the low-walled garden behind the adobe house, the patch of clay mixed in with sand and silt felt hard and dry under his bony buttocks. He ignored the ivory-coloured hair, long enough to drape over his unseeing eyes and bare shoulders, as well as the grizzled beard containing bits of last night's stew. His skin was bronzed and scarred by a thousand summer suns, and over his emaciated form he wore his usual torn, grey shorts and leather sandals, not knowing or caring if the neighbours were offended.

Even in a world where the steam engine dominated every aspect of life and culture, his contraption was a curiosity and a marvel of over-design. The main wheel was taken from the broken down wagon he once used to haul peat moss and manure home for his azaleas. He used a common iron steam boiler which could be heated by any fuel that would burn. The lead and brass piping he had scavenged from a condemned warehouse some months ago. The materials for the intricate gearing systems, cogs, pendulum, gear train, and escapement, were gifts of his departed wife's collection of clocks, which she had adored more than she did her husband. It was one of the many choices he made of which his three children did not approve.

However, mechanics alone would not provide the desired effect. It needed a special fuel in order to operate. The radium capsule would act as a catalyst, and combined with the exceptionally rare chemical compounds in the reaction chamber, once heated to the proper temperature, would allow him to achieve his long sought after goal.

It had cost Santiago his entire fortune, and reduced him to living in the gardener's hovel on their former estate so he could purchase the correct ingredients, substances so unique that they existed nowhere else on Earth. It would be worth it, though.

FLASH FICTION ADDICTION

"Yes, it will be worth it. I promise. You'll see," he murmured to himself in a way which convinced his children and neighbours that he was not quite sane. Pushing that thought aside he continued to work.

After it was all finished, and long after he had set the contraption into motion, and was granted his one great desire, many would say he should have wished for his sight to be returned instead or his fortune to be recovered. Santiago's dear Delphine was not always a pleasant woman, and when she discovered they were now paupers instead of wealthy, perhaps she would consider her life and his no longer worth living (which would be ironic given the circumstances).

However, he had forged the Reset Machine, which could be operated only once, in order to restore his departed spouse's life, gone these past fifteen years, and to cure her cancer. If she left him after that, well, for him it was still worth it.

"It was worth it. When you raise your words, you raise your ideals, and then your very soul. It was worth it. It was always worth it."

Once the machine was at its proper temperature and the cogs and wheels were all producing the necessary rotational speed, he pulled the wooden handle to activate the reset. There was the sound of thunder in the sky and the ground beneath him shook and spasmed like a woman in labour.

"But it is not the thunder that grows flowers, is it, Delphine?"

He could feel the air cool as the clouds moved above, and the first drops of rain fell upon his hoary head and blistered shoulders as the back door to the hovel opened and he heard her speak once again.

Price of a Soul
G. Dean Manuel

"Kid, keep your nose clean and study hard, you can be better than me even." Johnny patted my head.

I should've listened.

I idolised him, though. He was everything a poor kid dreamed of being. Mother who couldn't work, started hustling papers when he was five. At seven, organised the newsboys. With a word, half the city wouldn't get papers. The Fratelli's took notice. By nine, Johnny became the hub of the greatest spy network in New York.

Pretty soon, the streets of New York were his oyster and he was eating seafood every night.

He was what a poor kid looked up to. Closest thing to a hero. But every man with a statue is some sort of bastard. The world ain't black and white, and Johnny was nice but you can't run a criminal organisation with clean hands.

The day I realised Johnny wasn't a hero was like any other. It started with Leo the Candymaker. Leo loved kids. A bit too much, if you catch my drift. I didn't mind, gave us kids free taffy when we came by. One piece, then it was a pat on the butt.

That day, Johnny came in.

"Has my package arrived?" Johnny asked. When he saw me, he tipped the brim of his fedora. Class act. Didn't wonder why Johnny was waiting for a package there. Not too hard, leastways.

"Johnny," Leo spread his hands, "it's coming, I promise."

Johnny shrugged and pulled the toothpick from the corner of his mouth. "No problem, Leo." He took an Abba-Zaba bar, cracked it open, saw me, took another, and tossed it to me. "Don't forget, I know how *generous* you are with kids."

"I won't, Johnny. You'll have it soon."

"Come on, kid, got a job for you." Johnny led me outside. "Do you know Jake the Snake?"

I nodded. Everyone in the neighbourhood knew Jake the Snake. He went to prison for not squealing on a heist gone bad. He went down river a mean cuss, came back a stone cold killer.

"I want you to go to Luca's cafe and tell him that the candyman's a no show. He'll know what it means. Then tell him you get a hot meal." He pulled a dollar bill from his pocket and put it in my hand. "That's for you. Hide it, it's easy to lose at your age."

I wanted to admire it but Johnny was right. It didn't do to have money on display. I stuffed it into the pocket of my dirty pants. I took off running for Luca's cafe. In no time I found Jake on the patio. He was whittling wood, which seemed strange to me. You didn't see many people whittling wood.

"Quit staring, kid, your eyes'll pop out." A slice of the knife shaved off a thin piece of wood.

FLASH FICTION ADDICTION

I shook myself. "Johnny wanted me to tell you that the candyman was a no show and I get a hot meal."

"Sure, kid. Here," he tossed a menu, "order something."

I caught it and looked with eyes big as saucers. Barely knew how to read, just enough, so I was sounding out unfamiliar words.

Jake had called over a compatriot, Bruno, and they conferred in hushed tones. "Who's the midget?"

"Some kid that Johnny sent over." Jake still whittled. I could almost see it take shape.

"What's he doin'?"

"Johnny told him he could have a hot meal."

Bruno turned to me. "Kid, you like vegetables?"

I nodded. To be fair, as a street kid, I liked anything that was edible.

He nodded. Over his shoulder, he called, "Luca, get the kid some pasta fagioli, lasagna, and a couple of cannolis to finish him off." Bruno turned back to me, a wide smile across his face. "You're going to love this, kid." He reached down to muss my hair, his hand enveloped my whole head. "When I was you, this meal would've blown me away."

"Thanks, mister."

"Call me Bruno. You're part of the family now."

I would soon know what that meant. Never saw Leo again. I didn't pull the trigger but I killed him. I'd sold my soul for a hot meal and a dollar bill. Course, hindsight's 20/20. I'd like to think

I'd do different but I was a hungry street urchin. Thing is, I'd never figured my soul was worth that much...

After the Fall
Mary Wallace

"They say she used to have a body," she whispered to me as we stood on the beach. The faceless woman lay in front of us. "The old stories say she stood proud, holding a torch. She guarded the old world, before The Fall."

It was hard for me to take Eras seriously. She was always telling fanciful stories. I gave her a crooked smile. "A woman guarding the old world?" I scoffed. "Seems a little farfetched to me." I studied the faceless woman, avoiding Eras' annoyed gaze. Riling her ranked as one of my top amusements but I couldn't let her know that.

"Are you sure she wasn't just using that torch to cook dinner for her man? You know, the strong warrior?" I rubbed my chin as though in deep thought, considering this new possibility.

Eras' fist slammed into my stomach, knocking the wind from me, even as I fought against a burst of laughter. I fell over backward in the sand, exaggerating the force of her blow. As I lay there, I looked to where she stood above me, hands on hips glaring down at me.

"Get up, Tal," she said, rolling her eyes. "We have what we came for. If we hurry, we'll make it home before dark."

I sighed as I stood, silently admitting that the time for play was over. Eras and I shared a mutual fear of the dark. Our kind ruled the day but the nights belonged to the Thirst. It was practically suicide to be caught out after dark. "You hit like a girl," I said in a low voice. I ducked away, managing to avoid her swing.

She chased me for a short distance before we both gave up running and fell in beside one another, walking at a steady clip. Eras looked disappointed I didn't buy her story about the big faceless statue on the beach. We'd seen it a hundred times, just lying there. At high tide, the water swirled around the place her left eye should have been. Time and the elements had worn away whatever facial features she'd once had. No one really knew where she came from or whether she'd had a body once. Maybe before The Fall, she'd been a massive statue as Eras had been told. Perhaps she really had held a torch high above her head. The truth was that anyone who might know the truth of the statue was long dead. They'd all been killed in The Fall nearly a hundred years earlier.

Eras always wanted to know where things came from or why they were there. I was more practical. It didn't matter. I shook my head to chase away the thoughts Eras had planted in my mind. The past was behind us and what was important was surviving our own present. Right now, that meant taking the batteries we'd scavenged back home before it got dark enough for the Thirst to come out from their holes.

FLASH FICTION ADDICTION

The Thirst didn't come out when the sun was up. No one really knew why. There were stories. There were always stories. Someone was always telling someone else about the time they'd caught one and tied it up outside at dawn just to see what happened. Or the time they'd accidentally dug one up and watched it burst into flames when the sun touched its skin. I didn't buy any of those tales. I believed what I could see with my own eyes. I'd never seen one of the Thirst in the day and I never wanted to. I followed the rules and was inside the fence well before dark. The Thirst couldn't get past the electrified barrier and that was good enough for me.

Hush Little Baby
Ann Stolinsky

I bent down to hug my little girl, her hand attached to my pants leg. Tousling her blonde hair brought a smile to her face.

"Daddy, where are you going?"

"I'm sorry, Honey. Your mom and I don't want to live together any more, but you'll always be my little girl. I'll see you as often as I can, and I'll call you every night. We'll sing together before you go to sleep, OK? Just like we do now. Hush little baby, don't you cry, we'll sing it together." My breath caught in my throat.

"But Daddy," her lips quivered, and a pout emerged, "when will you colour pictures with me?" Her hand released my pant leg as she twirled from side to side. "I'm staying in the lines, just like you taught me. When will we colour together?"

"When I see you on the weekends, Honey, I promise. I'll buy you the biggest box of crayons I can find and we'll have lots of pictures to colour, I promise."

I couldn't say anything else. My throat was dry, only squeaks emerged. My little girl's eyes were filled with tears, as were mine. I slowly stood up, disentangled her arms from my legs, and walked toward the door.

"I love you, baby."

"I love you, Daddy."

* * *

That night, getting undressed for bed, I found a burnt sienna crayon in my coat pocket. I smiled, something I hadn't done for days. My baby gave me her favourite colour crayon. I lay down on my new bed, in my new bedroom, and cried.

The phone rang at midnight. Startled, I shook my head, disoriented from the unfamiliar surroundings. The phone rang again, and I reached for it.

"Is this Jim Roberts?" the unfamiliar voice asked. I grunted an assent. "Mister Roberts, I'm sorry to tell you that your wife and child have been in an accident. They're both at Highway Hospital."

"I'll be right there."

I grabbed the coat I had taken off and hung up just a few short hours ago, the one with the burnt sienna crayon in the coat pocket.

They both had passed on by the time I got there. Sitting by my baby's side in the hospital, the smell of crayons filled my senses. A strange bulge in her pants pocket caught my attention. I looked in her pocket to find the sky blue crayon, her second favourite. Tears flowed down my cheeks, for my estranged wife and for my baby, a child I would never see again.

I hugged her lifeless body and started singing. "Hush little baby, don't you cry..."

*   *   *

"Lieutenant, there's another one in here. This is bad. Is the ME here yet?"

"Not yet."

I walked into the room the detective indicated. It was a child's room, walls painted sky blue, a mural of a rainbow on the far wall, the white crib and chests of drawers stained red with spattered blood. A small desk sat off to the side, close to the far wall. The desk miraculously was spared from the blood spray. The detective was right, this was a bad one.

I leaned over the side of the stained crib. The baby lay on her back, dead eyes turned toward the ceiling, her blonde hair matted with clumps of dried red blood. Who could do this to a baby? My throat constricted.

The detective walked out of the room. My compulsion overcame me, and I couldn't help myself. I reached down to the crayons on the child's unblemished desk and grabbed several.

*   *   *

The door to my secret room creaked. The array displayed on the shelves within would get me booted off the force if anyone found it. The right wall was filled with objects taken from crime scenes involving adults, the left from crimes against children. As I gazed at my plunder, I was thankful the wall with the children's objects was less full than the other one.

I pulled the crayons from my pocket. Looking down, I realised what I was holding. I dropped the crayons on the floor. Collapsing next to them, tears flowed. The burnt sienna crayon was partially melted, probably because of the heat from being in my pocket. The smell and the colour brought me back to my baby, my beautiful little girl and my promise to her, to colour with her frequently. I sat down at the child's desk in my trophy room and began to colour, in the lines. Burnt sienna tree trunk and a sky blue sky. I quietly sang, "Hush little baby, don't you cry, Daddy's gonna sing you a lullaby."

Like Romeo and Juliet
S. Gepp

"We're like Romeo and Juliet."

"I hope not."

"What? Aren't we a romantic couple?"

"Of course. Our romance is wonderful and perfect. What's that got to do with Romeo and Juliet?"

"What? They were star-crossed lovers..."

"Their families hated each other. Our fathers might disagree politically but they're hardly drawing swords."

"Young lovers, then..."

"We're both twenty; neither of us is a fourteen year old."

"What they did was so romantic..."

"She pretends to commit suicide, he doesn't know, so he does commit suicide, and so then she does it anyway. So, miscommunication and over-reaction are obviously romantic."

"You take the fun out of everything."

Just You Wait
Kelli J. Gavin

I have to stop waiting. Stop wondering. Stop wanting. I don't think it serves a purpose anymore. The what if. The maybe. The possibly. It hurts more to hold onto all that never happened. I treasure the touch, the held hand, the embrace. But also the way you watched me. The way you smiled when I caught your eye. Those things happened, they are real. Absolutely mine for the keeping.

You moved on. I was alone and stuck where I am. You never changed your mind. Waiting, wondering and wanting, I am empty. No longer who I once was.

You wrecked me but you didn't break me. I am changed, stronger, I am new. I will be whole again. Just you wait.

Death Revenge
Feind Gottes

That bitch always said things would come back to bite me one day, Harvey thought casting out his fishing line. "The fish will be the only thing biting today! Oh, and the worms!" He burst out laughing at his morbid joke.

Harvey sat in his rickety boat waiting for a bite, trying to remember how he had ever ended up with that nasty woman. Aside from her being the only woman he'd ever found who would rub his willy—that he wasn't related to—he couldn't name a single redeeming quality about her. Excessive moonshine consumption had a little something to do with his foggy memory though it sure helped on the nights Robin had wanted more than a goodnight kiss.

The line of his pole jerked, interrupting his thoughts. Harvey held his breath staring at the line praying it hadn't been his imagination. Nothing moved, then, to his amazement, the line shook again. He had to move quickly to save his pole being pulled to the depths. He pulled back, snagging the hook into the beast. The fish pulled with such force it felt like he'd hooked a building.

The battle was on, man versus fish. Only one would claim victory. Harvey was determined to be that victor. He pulled with all his might doing his best to reel in the beast. The battle raged in deadlock, neither giving an inch.

Harvey's mind drifted to his late night devious deed. Robin had begun her incessant nagging the second he opened the door. She hit all the usual tropes about how all he did was drink all day while she did all the work, eventually drifting down to what a pathetic lover he was. Maybe it was the two quarts of moonshine or maybe something in his brain finally snapped, all Harvey knew was he had taken it long enough. The axe he used for chopping firewood began calling until he couldn't resist. Robin turned her back and he grabbed the axe burying it so deeply in the back of her skull he had to step on her neck to pry it out. Silence never sounded so good. He whacked her again to ensure the deed was done then buried her beneath the hydrangeas she hated so much.

Meanwhile, the battled raged on. Harvey knew he was slowly winning, though his strength was waning fast. His eyes nearly popped from his skull when the beast he'd battled for nearly two hours leapt out of the water. He had never seen a fish so huge. The excitement renewed his strength yet the battle continued. Nearly an hour later Harvey finally hauled the beast into his boat. It took whatever strength he had left. Victorious he yelled, then passed out cold, his catch at his feet.

Fog covered Harvey like a blanket when his eyes finally opened. He couldn't see the boat at his feet nor his hand in front of his face. Out of the fog a voice called his name. The blood drained from Harvey's face as Robin stepped out of the fog.

Worms squirmed their way through her hair, while spiders, centipedes and every other manner of insect scurried across her walking corpse. Harvey stepped back tripping over the seat.

"I told you the things would come back to bite you one day!" Robin cackled.

Harvey closed his eyes, praying it was some demented nightmare born of exhaustion and moonshine consumption. He screamed then opened his eyes, staring up at a full moon; his dead wife had disappeared. He laughed at himself, standing up to get a better look at the greatest catch ever.

Harvey needed both hands to lift the beast. He held it, enjoying the weight in his hands though unable to hold it up for long. Laying it back down, he caught his reflection in the water again. His image quickly shifted to that of his dead wife, she was smiling too. His jaw dropped as a centipede darted into her mouth.

"Come back to bite you!" she screeched.

Robin cackled as a pair of jaws shot up from the water. Recognition hit him as the alligator's jaws slammed shut over his head pulling him to the bottom. He could feel his head being crushed, worse, he could hear it, as the gator began its death roll. All Harvey could do was laugh at his dying thought, "The bitch was right, things came back to bite me!"

The Pain of Responsibility
P. A. O'Neil

"The nursery says your son is just a doll."

The ICU nurse jotted down the readings from all the various machines keeping Jane alive.

"There's been no change in Mrs Robinson's condition, so why don't you get some rest. I'll just be outside at the desk. Call me if you need me."

Luke sat dumbfounded as he watched the nurse perform the same routine every hour on his comatose wife. It seemed to him like they had been there for days not the few hours since the birth of their son. He blinked his eyes, once, then twice, then as the rhythm of the beeping monitors and the respirator filled his ears, he closed them for a third time.

"She's right—you look exhausted."

Luke opened his eyes wide as he recognised Jane's voice. He tried to rise, but found himself stuck, as if bolted to the chair.

"Don't try to get up, it's called Dream Paralysis—it's a kind of safety mechanism so you don't hurt yourself. Yes, this is a dream, but it's also me, Jane."

Luke's heart broke as he saw a smiling Jane, fully clothed, sitting on the end of the hospital bed, while simultaneously lying there, hair dishevelled, tubes pushing fluids in, others taking fluids out.

"I do look pretty bad, don't I?"

With his attention pulled back to his dream wife, he tried to ask her how she could be there; but as his mouth opened, no sound emerged.

"Am I a ghost? Well, no, not technically—I mean, I'm still alive—if you can call being kept on these machines living. It's why I'm here, Luke. I'm here to ask for you to let me go.

"Oh, I know you love me, and I love you too, my darling; but, this isn't fair, not for any of us... me, you, and certainly not for Michael. Sure, our son needs his parents, but right now, he doesn't even have one. I know you haven't been to see him since he was born."

Luke swallowed hard when faced with the truth of his neglect for his newborn son. He was holding Michael when Jane went into crisis with an aneurysm. He passed the baby off to a waiting nurse and ran to her bedside. He followed her to ICU, X-ray, and back to ICU, never farther than a few steps away. That was the previous evening. He looked at the visage of Jane, his eyes pleading for understanding.

"It's not your fault this happened. We both wanted a baby and knew it was a risk at my age. Now, it is time for you to let me go, but I'll never be far from you and our son. I will always love you."

FLASH FICTION ADDICTION

Luke watched as the healthy Jane approached, his lips moving soundlessly to beg her to stay. She reached out with one hand to gently push back hair fallen onto his forehead. It was a familiar gesture, one which had helped him know all those years ago that she was his missing half. He closed his eyes fearing her ghostly touch would be painful. When he opened them again, she was gone.

Luke looked around him, his head moving freely now, to see he was once again alone in the room with his ailing wife. His muscles were sore, a holdover from the paralysis, as he raised his hand to his head, the skin of his forehead and scalp tingled from where Jane's hand had been. Tears silently escaped his eyes as he looked at his empty hand, with them came the revelation of what he was supposed to do.

"Nurse!"

A Tick of Humanity
Kari Holloway

"I'm tired of trying to see the good in people." Susan rubbed her red-rimmed eyes, wanting to grind out the pain that continually seeped its way into her heart.

This year had been the hardest one of her career. It hadn't been about delivering puppies and routine procedures; it had been filled with discarded animals with leaking and oozing abscesses, cats tied in bags and dropped off bridges who were lucky enough to be rescued by a kayaker just to lose their broken and mangled legs and with them their chance of adoption, and rescues so starved that their hair was falling out and their bones looked like fossils dried in stone.

"You can't look at it like that," Doc said, as he slid down the wall and sat beside her. He pulled his stethoscope from around his neck. "Did you see little Betty Lou when she came in with her 4-H heifer? Now that heifer was just fine, after a few stitches and a round of antibodies, but because someone comforted that ten-year-old, someone listened to her, someone believed in her, she's gonna be one heck of a ring competitor. But you know what else? She's going to be one hell of a person."

Susan blew her nose. "That's just because she hasn't met a boy." It sounded petty, even to her ears, but she couldn't stop herself.

"What about Paone? That guy had never owned a cat before coming in with that squirrel. He watched you check that little thing over, and which cat was it... Roche... Rocko..." He snapped his fingers, trying to summon the name of the stray cat that had taken up residence.

"Rico. His name was Rico." Susan's head thumped against the concrete wall.

"That's the one. Rico. He started loving up on Paone, and by the time you finished that check-up, that man had decided to take the cat too. That was when you were a volunteer. Ten. Twelve years ago?" He waved his hand, dismissing time. "Point is, that guy still has that cat." Doc twisted the tubing.

"Don't forget Shady Grove. They had that complicated litter in the winter. If it wasn't for us, they would have lost the momma and those eight pups." Her fingers drilled against her knee.

"Yep. Driving on icy roads in the middle of a storm, we drove over there and did an emergency C-section right there in that lady's kitchen." He chuckled.

"What else was I supposed to do?" Susan's voice raised an octave, as she rubbed her cheeks.

Doc looked at her. His grey eyes soft. "Exactly what you did. You don't have to try to see the good in people. Why don't you try to see the good you bring into the world?"

The clock on the wall ticked. Through the frosted window, two shadows moved the next dog in a long line of loss and miracles. Behind the swinging door, the machines told of the life on the table.

"What are you going to do now?" Doc stood, wiping his hands on his pants, smeared with various shades of drying blood and iodine.

Susan braced her hand against the wall and stood. She reached for the scrubs on the metal rack. "You're right." She pushed through the door, pulling on the scrubs as she went. "You're right, Doc. You're always right."

The pit bull splayed on the table looked more like carcass than pet. Pieces of collar were embedded around his neck, consumed as the prison shrank and the prisoner grew. A back leg was twisted at an odd angle, leaving little doubt it was broken. His fur was gone in a bad case of road rash, leaving him a motley spectacle.

Her hand rubbed his rounded head. "You'll be fine, as long as we don't name you Cujo." She smiled, and her hands hovered over the embedded collar. Her gaze lingered on the broken leg. "Let's see if we can't save your leg while we're at it. Your sister's waiting for you in recovery. And if she can pull through, she doesn't want to hear how you couldn't hold on through this."

FLASH FICTION ADDICTION

Susan smiled a soft smile, finding the strength in talking to the incapacitated dog. "*Who knows,*" she mused, "*maybe I'll adopt you.*"

Michael

Justin Hunter

"Michael, it's time to get you ready for bed," James said. He was towelling off his son's wavy brown hair. Michael was seven years old, but acted a little young for his age. It wasn't like every seven year old still had his dad helping him wash. James has been seeing a bunch of kids with this undercut hairstyle of long hair on top and shaved close on the sides. He would make sure Michael got that cut. The kid had to start fitting in.

"Do I have school tomorrow?" Michael said.

"Yes. One more day and then it's the weekend."

"Can we go to the zoo?"

"I think so," James said, handing Michael his pyjamas. "I have some errands to run, but we could go there for a bit. We just can't stay all day."

"I don't want to go to school tomorrow," Michael said. James was looking at the dark circles under his boy's eyes. He wished he could get his boy to sleep better. James looked in the mirror and saw some pretty baggy circles under his own.

"School is something you have to do," James said. "I have to go to work. You have to go to school. How else can you expect to get a great paying job so you can send me money when I get old?" Michael laughed. It was an old joke to them both, but it made them feel warm inside.

"What about the money you make at your job?" Michael said.

"I've spent that money frivolously on things like electricity and food. I will never learn. Maybe instead of the zoo we could go bet on some horses."

"Mom wouldn't like that," Michael said.

"Mom wouldn't like it if we left her home," James said. "She's our good luck charm." Michael struggled into his clothes and went to the sink to brush his teeth.

"How long until mom comes home?" Michael said.

"A couple more weeks. She has to finish up the orientation for the new employees. Then she should be home for at least a month before she has to leave again."

"Good," Michael said. James was glad that Michael didn't say such things in front of his mom. Toni worked a hard job and made good money. She hated to be away from the family, but that was the job. James did his best to not make her feel guilty for being gone, that it was a necessary sacrifice for the family, but he couldn't stop the guilt she put on herself.

"Do you think you'll sleep okay tonight?" James said.

"I don't know. I feel a little weird."

"Good weird or bad weird?"

"A little bad. I feel like there is a hole in my stomach"

"What's in the hole?" James said. He picked up Michael and gave him a big hug.

"It's a small hole, but there's lots of things inside. The hole is small, but it's deep. It goes for miles and miles." James lifted Michael high and kissed him on the stomach. Michael laughed.

"I fill the hole with love and kisses," James said.

"The kisses go into the hole," Michael said. "But the things eat them. Dad, I'm scared."

"Don't be scared," James said. "Everybody sleeps."

"Even the animals? Even Fish?"

"Even the animals and every fish in the sea." James brings Michael into his room and lays him gently down on the bed.

"I don't think the things in my stomach go to sleep. I can feel them. I can always feel them."

"How about a bedtime story?"

"There is no time," Michael said. "You need to hurry." James looked into Michael's eyes as the pupils dilated until there was no white to be seen.

"Tonight is going to be bad?" James said, sounding to himself like he was the child and Michael the adult.

"Tonight is going to be bad. I'm sorry, daddy." The fingernails on Michael's hands began to lengthen. James reached under the bed and brought out leather straps. He put Michael's arms into them gently and pulled the straps as tightly as he dared.

"Not tight enough," Michael said.

"I'll hurt you if I make it any tighter."

"I'll hurt *you*, daddy."

"No tighter," James said. "That's it."

"Lock the door," Michael said. "Go now."

James got up from the bed. His child was beginning to shake.

"You have to go before I wake up," Michael said.

"You're not asleep..."

"I'm about to wake up. They are coming out of the hole. I can't stop them." James ran from the room and shut the door. He locked it from the outside with a key and closed the deadbolt he installed several months ago when this started happening.

He heard his child groan. They were coming.

Pumpkin's Purpose
Emily Fluckliger

Nothing would delight Pumpkin more than to be a carriage again. When the blonde girl in her silken dress picked him up, Pumpkin knew he'd found a home. The others would transform into faces that glowed, but he'd be carved into an image of his past. The thick orange skin fading to pure white, the seeds stretching and curling into iron coils and spirals.

Of course, he wouldn't be a real carriage, not ever again. Instead, Pumpkin would still be a squash, a squash who'd pass on in the form of his greatest achievement. The girl would create twists and swirls from his orange flesh, and once he shrivelled, and life ended, all could remember him as the carriage.

This girl even looked like the princess. Though Pumpkin knew he must be dreaming, his lofty aspirations taking him into the clouds. *Pumpkins belong on the ground*, the gardener had said.

She skipped and hopped cradling the heavy vegetable in both arms. Her white teeth glittered like crowns upon the head of a royal. Though her dress snagged on weeds and dirt dusted the skirts, the girl still galloped. She carried him from the field and into her courtyards. The pathway of stones that lined the gardens reminded Pumpkin of a place he'd once been.

If Pumpkin could puff a chest and poke a nose into the air, he would. Pumpkin waited. The patch had taught him patience, the carriage; honour and glory. The girl returned with a knife and spoons. She crossed her legs and pulled Pumpkin into her lap. He rested on a bed of silken skirts. She cut a hole at the top, severing Pumpkin's stem. While she scooped out his seeds Pumpkin would have laughed, if he could. It tickled.

The girl stuck out her tongue. Pressing it to the side of her mouth, she finally began carving. The knife twisted and cut creating a crescent moon pointing toward the sky. She bent her arm to carve circles above. *Wait!* The shapes she sculpted formed a face. Pumpkin expected better, he dreamt of glory, he hoped for the body of a carriage.

Pumpkin had eyes now, with which to cry. But he waited, perhaps patience was more valuable than glory. The girl lifted Pumpkin to meet her face. They stared at one another. Pumpkin saw a glimmer in her, the same face of the princess, only younger and with a bit of someone else... Her lips spread into a smile while her cherub face flushed red from the work.

Pumpkin needed no candle to warm him. The girl's face gave him all the glory he'd hoped for, her delight; an eternal honour. Pumpkin returned the smile. This he could do. He shared her joy with a smile he'd keep forever.

"Princess! The kingdom's trick or treating has begun," a familiar voice called from the castle window.

With his newly gifted eyes, Pumpkin looked up for a final glimpse of the queen he'd once served.

Bombshell
Matthew Stevens

That morning I knew the world was different. My shelter had no windows, yet I could sense the change outside. The sound of the bombshell being dropped had yanked me from a dead sleep. But I didn't understand how drastically the environment could be transformed.

I tapped a few buttons on the panel next to the door. The computer beeped calculating the quality of the atmosphere outside. A small green light and a pleasant ding signalled that despite the unseen changes to the landscape, the air was safe to breathe.

The seal hissed as I turned the wheel and the pressure equalized. Somehow the very smell of the air had changed. A cloud of dust sucked in, billowing around me. With a shove and a groan, the door swung outward.

Any expectations I had were obliterated by the scene laid out before me. When I was young, Hollywood went through a phase of post-apocalyptic movies. They showed two possibilities. One: a barren brown landscape, dust clouds swirling across the horizon, skeletons of trees dotting the area, a capricious vulture perched on an arbitrary branch. The other: a city with buildings full of blown-out windows and small fires still burning random piles of people's lives.

What I saw was neither. I checked the readout again. The colours were wrong, all wrong, as if I had woken up colour blind. Green was red, brown was blue, and the sky shone a burnished gold. Every manmade structure had been replaced with a hive shaped edifice of similar size and shape; they varied from short and squat to tall and cylindrical.

The bombshell that had dropped hadn't destroyed everything as predicted. In the blink of an eye the world had been terraformed. Not far from the entrance to my shelter lay the carcass of the machination that had delivered this change from some unknown place. The fuselage was the only thing of the surroundings reminiscent of those post-apocalyptic Hollywood imaginings: blackened and smoking with a few arbitrary tongues of flames burning through holes in the hull.

We knew it was coming. It was inevitable. World leaders prepared us as best they could, but no one knew when or how it would come. They only held the certainty that change would arrive. And violently.

I heard her shoes clink on the metal floor behind me. Soon her hand rested gently on my shoulder. I could see her in my peripheral vision as she moved next to me.

"I..." she started, but words failed her.

"Yes," I said, answering her unspoken question. "This is still home."

"How can you tell?"

I pointed out landmarks, although they now had different skins. She nodded in recognition.

"Are we the same? Even if this place is not?"

I took her hands. She turned towards me. Our eyes met.

"We're not. Because this can never be the same." My gaze led her eyes out over the world that now surrounded us.

"If that's true, what do we do now? What's next?" Her concern was palpable.

"We do what we've always done." I squeezed her hands and we left the shelter behind walking toward what had been the city we had known so well only the night before. "We survive."

We set off to explore, to learn, and to find a way to make sense of it all.

"Together."

Kink

Brian Rosenberger

He was a man of questionable taste and unquestionable wealth. A self-made millionaire.

Acquiring knowledge of the brothel was the cost of an airplane.

Entrance to the brothel was the cost of an airline.

Fortunately, he owned several airlines.

Inside the brothel was an orgy of feathers and fins, tentacles and tails, claws and horns, fur and scales.

He only had eyes for her. She had compound eyes. Big, round and beautiful.

Money gained him entrance but money couldn't buy everything.

The cancer was killing him. Not treatable. He had other ideas.

The mantis smiled and gently took his hand.

A Mama's Love
D. M. Burdett

Dark clouds sprawled across the sky and a hot wind billowed in from the thrashing sea as the brassy glare of a coming storm drained colour from the horizon.

The wind whipped sand into clouds as Rel watched his mama scream into the skies, a small bundle clutched to her breast. Her ragged clothes and long dark hair billowed angrily around her as she knelt in the barren sand. He looked away, across the ocean, as lightning flashed across the heavens as if it too grieved for the child.

After moments that seemed endless, her wails subsided and Trea crouched beside her.

"Mama?" she whispered softly.

Trea took the swaddled infant from her mama's arms, cradling him in her own one last time, before she gently placed him into the grave. Mama lifted a handful of dirt and let it slowly trickle over the worn cloth before Rel shovelled earth back into the hole. "The Gods have him now," Mama sobbed.

Addi had made the grave-marker. A simple floppy drive blanking plate that had the baby's name scratched into it, marked his brother's final resting place next to his father. The eldest and youngest of the T'anu family would forever lie together. Addi staggered and coughed bloody phlegm as he bent to push the spike into the soft ground.

Addi will be next, Rel thought sadly as he turned and followed the rest of his family back across the wet sand.

He pulled back the magnetic-tape curtain that covered the entrance to their cliffside home and ducked inside. The fire flicked shapes across the rock where the warmth couldn't penetrate.

Rel scowled at the small fish that Trea was preparing. "One fish can't feed a whole family."

"It soon will," Trea said, and she looked over at Addi as another cough wracked his body and Mama muttered soothing words into his ear, her hand on his hot brow.

They were both wrong.

*   *   *

Rel woke from a fitful sleep as Mama whispered in his ear.

"Quickly, Rel. Come outside," she said, urgently.

Rel pulled his tattered blanket around his shoulders and followed her.

The low sun cast long shadows across the beach, and he stepped into the shade of a man sitting atop a desert beast. The camel snorted as the man held tight to the reins, his dusty fedora pulled down over his eyes.

"What's going on, Mama?" Rel's eyes moved from the man to Mama.

"This is my son. Rel of T'anu. You can pay him." Mama squinted up at the man.

The man unbuckled his side bag, pulled out a small purse, and threw it down to Rel who caught it with one hand. Feeling its heaviness, Rel looked down at the pouch.

The scripted symbol of the Resurrectionists ran through the lush dark fabric in fine gold thread. Cold sweat pricked the back of Rel's neck, and he looked up at the beast's load.

The animal carried skin bags that hung from a wooden frame. Blood had seeped through—the body parts wrapped untidily inside them—and flies darkened the air around them. The Resurrectionist's journey had been prosperous.

"You sold Addi to the Resurrectionists, Mama?" He spoke in hushed, angry tones. "How could you?"

"Not Addi, Rel. He's come for me."

Rel gasped. "No, Mama!"

"Rel, listen-"

"No, Mama. You don't need to do this. We can manage!" He spoke in quick, pleading bursts, his hands gripped Mama's arms.

"The deal is done," the Resurrectionist interrupted. "I gave a good price for the live specimen." A smile touched his face but not his eyes.

"You're not taking her!" Rel spat.

The Resurrectionist shrugged. "If you renege, I'll take you both. Dead."

"Hush, Rel." Mama spoke softly. "It is done."

Hot tears began to run down Rel's face and Mama cupped his cheeks in her hands and pulled his face to hers.

"Look after my babies, Rel. You are their father now."

"What have you done, Mama?" Rel whispered.

"You can buy medicines for Addi. And food."

"I can't be a man, Mama. I can't!"

"You already are a man, Rel." She kissed the top of his head and turned to the Resurrectionist. She raised her arms to him, and he pulled her frail body up onto the beast. Mama held tight to the Resurrectionist's back as he yanked the reigns and the beast turned slowly.

"Mark a grave for me, Rel," Mama shouted over her shoulder as the camel galloped away.

At that moment, Trea ran from the shack and fell into Rel's arms. "Addi has gone to the Gods," she sobbed.

Rel dropped to his knees, his arms still wrapped around his sister.

He watched the horizon until the beast disappeared into the sun's haze.

The Boogeyman
C. L. Williams

"The boogeyman is in my room!" Billy screams as he attempts to get his mum's attention.

She comes to the door. "Honey, the boogeyman isn't real".

"He's real, I swear!" Billy cries hysterically to his mother.

"There is no boogeyman, Billy, go to bed," his mum says as she closes the door behind her.

Billy sinks into his bed as his closet door opens, the boogeyman reveals himself to Billy and asks, "She still doesn't believe you?"

"No," Billy says in anger.

"How about this?" the boogeyman says, making Billy an offer. "Tell her to check your closet, if she looks inside, you get some cookies."

"What if she doesn't see you when she checks the closet?" Billy asks.

"Not all parents see me. All she needs to do is open the closet. Now give it a go one more time," the boogeyman says as he goes back into Billy's closet.

"Muuum!" Billy screams. "The boogeyman is in my closet!"

Billy's mum comes up once more, this time more frustrated than the last. She angrily opens the door. "Billy, the boogeyman is *not* real, go to sleep."

"Will you at least check my closet. If you check, I promise I will go to sleep and I won't call you anymore," Billy says, trying to bargain.

"*Fine*," Billy's mum says as she goes to check his closet. She opens the door and the boogeyman is standing right in front of her. However, the blank look on her face proves that he is only visible to Billy.

"No boogeyman. You made me a promise young man," she tells him trying to make sure Billy goes to sleep.

"I know, I won't call for you anymore. Goodnight mum. I love you," Billy says.

"Goodnight." She goes over to his bed to give him a kiss. "I love you too Billy, now get some sleep." Billy's mum closes the door behind her.

"She's gone, you can come out now," Billy tells the boogeyman.

"I wish she could've seen me, the looks I get when parents can see me," he tells Billy as he exits the closet with the jar of cookies he promised. He hands Billy a cookie. Billy quickly takes it from the boogeyman's hand and starts chowing down.

"If you don't mind me asking," Billy says, "why do monsters hide in closets just to give kids cookies?"

"Well, Billy, we need to fatten you up before we eat you," he says as he grins at Billy. A now frightened Billy drops his cookie as the boogeyman starts laughing. "I'm kidding, we monsters are vegetarians, we just like sharing stuff," he tells Billy as he pulls a cookie out of the jar and joins Billy in a midnight snack.

High Space
Simone Cristiano

Jackson opened his eyes and stared at the ceiling of his cabin, waiting for his mind to start functioning properly before trying to move out of his bed. He instantly noticed that the light inside the room was weaker than the day before.

Oh for God's sake, the generator is dying again! he thought while brushing back his hair with his hands.

He slowly turned on his right side, he pushed himself up and sat on the bed with his back leaned against the wall, whilst looking at the time on the holographic clock on the bedside table.

"Jesus Christ! It's already ten thirty. I'd better hurry up," he said to the empty room.

His morning routine was always exactly the same. He always woke up no later than 9am, had a shower and a coffee and walked up to the communication room on the second deck of the spaceship. After trying to contact NASA for two hours, he ran tests and maintenance tasks until four o'clock.

The rest of his day was working out and vaping liquid weed, commonly known as BEE. Jackson was the only survivor, out of 350 passengers on the Theseus X-34, a helium mining ship on his way back to Earth from Jupiter. An unknown virus wiped out the entire crew in less than two weeks, after only a month of travel back to Earth.

It killed everyone but Jackson and he believed that, somehow, BEE made him immune. He was the only one on the ship crazy enough to sneak on board a five years supply. Certainly the most brilliant mining engineer in the world, that had in mind to stash his juice in the only thing that the space agency wouldn't have been able to see inside of: USBH, Uranium battery packs for Shredders, the atomic mining guns used to cut the solid helium close to Jupiter's core. As Jackson knew exactly how many batteries they needed in the process, he'd managed to get his hands on the backup crates that would never be used.

Even though he learned how to fly the spaceship, following radio instructions from NASA in his first months alone, after the incident in an asteroid field, many of the main guiding systems were permanently damaged. His only hope to get home was restricted to two engines, the emergency pilot cockpit and the short range radio station, which Jackson managed to wire into the main aerial, but without any apparent effectiveness. Another day on board was about to come to an end. Another day, alone, in the dark nothingness of space. Loneliness was no longer a problem though for the stoned engineer. During all of these months, exercising was what kept Jackson fit, getting stoned was what kept him sane, or at least that's what he was inclined to think. Pondering on life, sat on the couch in the main lounge, Jackson was about to enjoy the last vape of the day when he realised that he was out of BEE.

"Fuck! Not now!"

He stood up and started walking towards Section 28, where his juice was stored inside the batteries. After a good ten minutes he came back to the lounge and sat again on the couch, ready to get his last treat. He loaded up the little cartridge in the side slot of his vape, pressed the button and started breathing in *God's Gift*.

As soon as the warm vapour entered his lungs he felt his brain slowing down, his hands becoming mellow, and his mind getting placid and quiet again after the stressful unplanned walk. All of sudden, though, he realised that something was wrong. He couldn't breathe. He was choking.

Jackson jumped up in panic, coughing heavily he started spitting bile on the floor. His heartbeat increased rapidly, his skin started burning, and his eyes began to flood with blood.

Uranium! That fucking thing must have cont... Jackson fainted before finishing his thought and fell heavily on the floor, dying slowly in a puddle of vomit and blood. That last lust cost him his life, after months of lonely pleasure, *God's Gift* turned its back on him. A damaged battery, an invisible Uranium leak, a single breath and his life was over. Alone, in the dark nothingness of space, his entombed body would cruise forever in an endless journey towards nowhere.

Death of a Head Hunter
Hákon Gunnarsson

Joe hadn't been shooting for a while. Not since Maggie died. It wasn't the same without her. You see, that's how they met in the first place, shooting for the Head Hunters, hunting people, that's what they did in their spare time. I'm sorry, I just realized that I may be giving you the wrong idea. The Head Hunters was just the name of the group they belong to. They didn't kill anyone, or bring them to justice.

They were street photographer, taking pictures of people, trying to get their stories in the frame. That was the game, and it was important to them. Maggie had always been better than him. He knew that. Or maybe it was just that they had different styles. He was a purist, would never do anything to change the scene. He shot from the hip, letting the camera hang around his neck in the strap, he would level it with one hand, and use the remote control in his pocket to take the picture. When he did it right, the only thing that could give it away was the sound of the camera, but the street sounds muffled it out. Most of the time people didn't know they'd been photographed. It was like they had been shot by a ghost.

Maggie did things differently. She would let anyone know she was taking pictures, raised the camera to her eye if she wanted to take a picture, and sometimes she talked to people she wanted to photograph. In fact, that was what she was best at. Talking to people. Joe remembered this one time. They met a guy that was living in the homeless shelter, and she wanted to take his picture, but he even though he was fine with talking to them, he was wary of the camera, but Maggie just continued to talk and take pictures until she got one that was really good.

He missed talking to her. He missed eating with her. He missed sleeping with her. He missed living with her. He missed her. All he had left of her was a stack of photos he had taken of her, and boxes upon boxes of photos she'd taken of other people. No matter who good they were, they weren't Maggie. Days, weeks, months had passed and his passion for photography was as dead as she was.

Then one day he got talking to Mark, a friend from the group, who told him he might be wrong. They had shared this passion, so maybe he could get closer to her again by getting back into the game. Joe wasn't sure, he doubted it, but was willing to give it a shot. So he took to the streets, and photographed some people. It wasn't enjoyable, his heart wasn't in it, but somehow he took a few dozen shots.

In the evening he uploaded the photos onto his computer to have a look, more out of habit, than interest. Joe looked at the first photo, and got a jolt. The composition was right. The lighting was right. The subject was interesting. But there, in the background, he could see Maggie. She was dead. He knew that.

FLASH FICTION ADDICTION

He'd had to go to identify her, and then bury her. And despite all that, there she was. It had just been someone like her. Yes, that was it, he told himself. Then he turned to the next one, and there she was again. Slowly he went through all the photos he'd taken that day and she was in most of them. And yet, she couldn't have been there.

Joe just sat there, took a deep breath, and looked out of the window. He could see the warmth of the sunset. A fact, the night was coming. A fact, she was gone. With that in mind, he went through his photos again. Then again. And a few times after that. By dawn he could have described every single photograph in details, but he'd also noticed something. Maggie was talking in all these photos, and in real life she'd known better than to enter a shot like that. She was telling him something. Finally he realized what it was. He closed the computer, and went to bed. A couple of days later he went out into the street again to hunt for more people to take photographs of.

"Excuse me, I couldn't help noticing that magnificent beard, may I take a portrait of you?"

Beauté Folle
Amanda R. Woomer

"What a beautiful colour!"

"So deep!"

"Luscious, even!"

The prima ballerina smiled as she made her way to her dressing room.

Slamming the door shut behind her, she ignored the muffled scream of the young ingénue she had tied to her sink.

The girl's pale white skin was covered in cuts—some old and scabbing, some new and still bleeding.

Wiping the old, dull red from her lips, the prima ballerina stood up and tiptoed over to the girl, a silver knife clutched in her hand.

"They love my new colour," she purred as she knelt down before the trembling girl. "But it's not quite what I'm looking for."

Without a word, she sliced the girl's throat, the bright red blood splattering her face.

Standing to look in the mirror, the prima ballerina rubbed her finger along her lips, painting them a deep, vicious red.

She smiled. Finally, it was the perfect colour.

"They'll love it."

Passengers

Jo-Anne Russell

They look like us with clouded eyes, their knowledge far surpassing ours. They wander our ship, unwanted passengers, as we return home. Our arrogance was their gateway and will be our demise.

Through thick glass I stare at the stars—our greatest adventure becomes our worst nightmare. I program in a new course and feel the ship shift direction. Communication with home is now lost.

Outside the bridge I hear them working, trying to get inside. It will be too late by the time they get in.

I smash the panel and give the human race another day, another chance.

We Shall Survive
John Tuttle

Survival. To us, that is our life, an instinct, a base desire, a necessity, our supreme task which is to be carried out on a daily basis throughout our measly, diminutive lifespans. Survival. It is what we have done for ages upon ages, as long as the past can be recalled. It is the concern of all our people.

So long ago we retreated from the Earth we knew, once a world of fresh air and light, to beneath its dusty surface. There deep under the ground our ancestors grew accustomed to the bareness, the dryness, and most of all the darkness. Here we still dwell to this very day, and we will outlive those who read our tracks and this message too.

Survival. It shall continue. We are scavengers, defenders, caregivers. Now we are forced to dispatch small parties to return to the world above in search of rations for the colony. The verdure of vegetation has returned, and the sun remains unchanged. Much is edible there, but the surface hosts many dangers as well. Other creatures dwell there.

Massive giants they are; aliens or hybrids we are not sure. But they are not of our kind. We are well-built, physically strong, but in the face of the giants we are so easily snuffed out. Even those of us who have learned to take to the air are not swift enough to evade them.

We eat of fruits, and the splendid rarity of meat is attained when we stumble upon the remains of a larger creature's meal. We gather. We consume. But we are also to store away a portion in preparation for the cold quiet months which await.

The colony is made up of many races, yet the mindset of each one is identical: survival. Our queen, mother and leader, is greatest of all. Our heritage is far more grand than our present lot. We admire the ancients of another continent who so boldly endeavoured to construct safe havens which reached high into the sky, while we lowly ones tunnel in dirt.

Her royal highness assigns everyone a task for which he is fit. We have builders, miners, scouts, nurses, soldiers. My responsibility is that of head of one of our militaristic forces. I am a leader of defenders, and we will fight if need be. We know we must do what we must so as to protect the upcoming generation, in order to survive.

Why do we do this you ask? Ants we are, small creatures of the earth! Objects many times our own weight are simple to move. We eat, and we protect in order to survive, thriving on the dying and the things you leave behind. We burrow into the dirt; there the queen of ants gave birth to the colony. Many, many other colonies are there throughout this world.

Our distant relatives of the African continent, termites, build tall buildings of red soil which solidifies as if adobe. And other cousins in other countries make homes of canopies from leaves up in the trees, and still others construct mounds, giant hut-like structures, in their golden meadows. We defend and scavenge. Yet we will destroy and take. We cut down, burrow, and build up. We take over, and we bring with it change. Wherever we go we adapt and adapt the landscape too to assure our survival. We ants will always continue to adapt. We shall survive.

Ragged Claws
Zachary Sparks

It started slow at first, nothing drastic. Fishermen reported record numbers of crabs in their catches; hauled in by nets or traps, clinging to the lines, it didn't matter. We sent vessels to the depths to study this surge in numbers. We thought the environment was bouncing back, that we had turned a corner and the oceans that birthed us could support us once again. But those were the wrong answers because we weren't asking the right questions. The sea level began to fall, inches at first, then feet. Welcome news to our threatened coastal cities, but distressing on a global scale. We noticed when the crabs appeared elsewhere, when they scuttled across the deserts and slid through our cities, but still we did not ask the right question. We asked, 'Where are they coming from?' We should have asked, 'Where are they going?' We know the answers to both now.

Crabs began appearing faster and faster, but it always seemed to happen just out of sight. In our labs and our libraries we searched for answers, but only found more crabs. We would glance away from our lab benches to study our results and when we returned our gaze we found fewer beakers and more crabs. We consulted the card catalogue and found crabs in place of the books we wanted. The universe is a vast ocean and the nature of reality is tidal. As it ebbs, everything is scrambling and scuttling to get off the naked beach of the universe for fear of what may stoop to scoop them up.

We are stranded—those of us left—in the remaining tide pools, too afraid of the unreality of becoming crabs, frightened of whatever is coming to fish us... out.

Will
Andrew J. Lucas

I should have known better than to go to the reading of the will. Twenty years hadn't mellowed the old man—even in death he was a total bastard. When that pencil necked lawyer trotted out the tablet with the e-will and that fancy Wi-Fi enabled pen I should have just turned around and walked right out.

The old man and I didn't have much of a relationship when I was a kid. Always engrossed in writing his next novel no time for a son. The situation certainly didn't improve when I left for the Marines. Sure, it was the cyber corps and all three of my deployments were served in Tallahassee riding herd on drone swarms over the Yemen. Booyah! Today's army doesn't need stereotypical soldiers, no sir. No chiselled pecs on me. The Corps wanted me for my brain, not my body, and that just didn't sit well with the old man. He figured I was wasting my time and my potential—bastard was so smug when I was cashiered.

Been about fifteen years since I've seen the old man, enough time to earn three stripes, settle down with a nice girl and have a couple of kids. Of course, that was before the accident. Blew out the part of my medulla oblongata that allowed a cyber-marine to control a flight of combat capable drones from a continent away. I left with a small medical pension, muscle tremors and in debt up the eyeballs. The wife was working double shifts at the VA, and I fell into writing features for the local webpaper—must have inherited some of the old man's talent.

Now I don't miss the old man, not a bit. Only reason I'm here is to see if the old bastard left me anything. Selfish? Sure but anything to get this crippling debt off my back.

Turns out the old man was loaded, invested in some high tech neuro-net stock before the government nationalized all that stuff. Good of the nation, national security and all that. Anyways, he'd made out like a bandit, had a cool half million according to the lawyer, and it was all mine for the taking. A windfall like that would not only clear my debt but set me up to fulfil what I really wanted to have—the freedom to write. I've had that bug since I was a teen, it was part of the reason we'd butted heads so much. He was a national treasure, a living legend I could never live up to, though it didn't stop me from trying.

Papers were pretty standard, only stipulation was that I wouldn't get any of the money unless I used his favourite pen for all my affairs, writing included. Crazy old goat had lost it. Still—half a million dollars... I took the pen and signed.

'Are you sure you want to use the passive voice there, son?" my father's voice said, emanating from the pen.

The Elephant in the Room
Lincoln Lally

On a little futon amongst a litter of cigarette papers and empty tea cups curled a little pair of lovers. Cardboard squares of lust in their bellies and a quiet acoustic playlist played from somewhere on the floor.

The key to this affair was not to mention it, so they kept their x-files and the demons that emerged for the daylight only and found a quiet corner in each other.

One week separated them and she wondered if he smelt the other guy on her or if the reason he smelt so good was because of a well spent morning with another before she rolled into town. She could never know, and they'd never asked; skirting at the edges of definition, happy to leave the curtain perfectly intact.

He asked her, "Do you mind if I roll a smoke?"

"No, go ahead." She was mournful of his warmth that he took when he left the curled comfort of the couch.

The acid was wearing thin but the light from the lamp still danced and she couldn't quite make sense of the shadows in the rip of his pants.

She wondered what she liked about men, really. Her lover yesterday was much hungrier and there was so much comfortable silence between these two now.

He rolled a cigarette and sat on the bench, not bothering to ask if it was okay to smoke inside.

"So my friend Andy, the tattooist guy, he was telling me about this Japanese guy he's tattooing. And he's missing the pinky finger, like they do in the Yakuza."

"That's where the pinky promise thing comes from. It's Japanese." She shrugged, she thought she'd mentioned that she spent a year in Japan with university.

He raised his eyebrows and lit the smoke. The smoke drifting up through his fringe and onto the peeling ceiling above.

She wanted to press between his legs, hoping for his free hand on her hip but they weren't these kinds of lovers. Yesterday was different and she needed to put that out of her mind, no matter how many times the image of the other man's finger in her mouth busted into her head.

"I don't think I've ever made a pinky promise." He blew out the smoke. "Maybe as a kid, over like money for lollies of something."

"I've made lots, but I used to take them very seriously. I pinky promised my first boyfriend I'd love him forever. Only one I remember breaking."

He looked at her, there was a little judgement lurking there when she managed to catch his gaze. He could never keep eye contact, he offered the smoke and she jumped, the clock struck four.

Karma's a Bitch
Hanorah Papa

Terrified yelps abruptly woke Karma from her afternoon nap. Badmaster roughly grabbed her terrified litter of puppies and one by one tossed them into a large sack.

Alerted to their cries, Karma bolted towards Badmaster, barking and baring her teeth. She attempted to attack him only to have the rope around her neck tighten, jolting her to a standstill. Desperately, Karma strained on the rope, her barking angering Badmaster.

"Shut up Karma or you'll be next, you stupid mongrel." He shouted, pulling the sack closed. "You know I mean it girl. You won't remember them tomorrow anyway and I don't need extra mutts around the place."

He tied the one end of a long rope around the neck of the sack and dragged the whimpering puppies to the edge of a dried out well in the middle of the farmyard.

Hearing the pups cry, Karma barked louder and pulled on the rope that was securely attached to an old wooden stump.

Reaching the well, Badmaster cursed in an attempt to lift the heavy, wriggling sack and drop it into the opening of the well.

Sensing the imminent danger to her babies, Karma tugged with all her strength on the rope, yelping in pain as it burned into her neck before snapping and setting her free.

She wildly flew at Badmaster, sinking her teeth into his calf, making him scream in agony.

"Get away from me Karma, you crazy mutt. You're next." He cried out, dropping the sack to protect himself.

The rope around the sack unravelled, setting the puppies free.

"Damn it. Get back here you mangy animals."

Karma's instinct told her to continue her attack on Badmaster, who tried in vain to defend himself. Taking one step back, he tripped over the sack, losing his footing. Karma and Badmaster's eyes locked for a split second before he fell headlong into the well. A loud crack of his head and neck put an end to him.

Sniffing the air, Karma was satisfied the danger to her precious puppies had passed. She turned from the well and greeted her ecstatic babies with a triumphant bark.

After the initial excitement of their happy reunion, Karma and her babies settled under a shady tree, for a well deserved feed and sleep, free at last from Badmaster.

Sisters

S. B. Rhodes

The bond between siblings is a strange thing. Some siblings are joined at the hip, while others are their own biggest rivals. For Abigail and Olivia Manchester, it was the latter. They had not always been so distant. In fact, their mother loved to remind them during each of their arguments that they were best friends from the very beginning, even holding hands in their ultrasound.

However, their friendship was put to the test more than a few times over the years, starting with minor issues and escalating to all-out war. Before long, they had stopped talking altogether, and it seemed that any hope of rekindling their friendship was lost forever. Then tragedy struck, and now they were forced to pick up the pieces.

* * *

Olivia sat on the sofa, looking at the photo of her mother and father on their wedding day. "We'll never see them again," she said, tears streaming down her face. She thought back to the night that everything changed, Christmas Eve.

Family had come down for the holidays, and Aunt Sophia attempted to make small talk. "You must have to beat the boys off with a stick," she said. "Are you seeing anyone?"

Olivia overheard Abigail excitedly telling her about David and stormed out of the room. Despite the predetermined sleeping arrangements, she could no longer handle bunking with her sister. So, she grabbed her things and moved into the basement until she could get her own room back.

Her mother called after her, but she did not want to hear it. She just wanted to be alone. Unfortunately, her wish was granted. Now the only person she had left in the world was her sister. She wished she could see her mother again and talk to her about how she was feeling.

"Oh, mom," she said sadly as she walked through the house, with its ash-covered floors and singed walls. She touched the fireplace. This is where it started.

Their little cousin, Aaron, had awoken in the middle of the night to get a glass of water. On his way back, he tripped over an extension cord, causing the dancing Santa to fall over into the fireplace. In his half-asleep state, he did not realize what was happening and went back to sleep. By the time firefighters arrived, the entire house was engulfed in flames.

* * *

FLASH FICTION ADDICTION

Abigail sat in her room, holding the promise ring David had given her as a gift just before Christmas break. She held it to her chest as she thought back to the night of the Winter dance. She had attempted to be discreet when sneaking out of the auditorium to see him.

She did not mean to hurt her sister, but they had fallen for each other. She will never forget the look of betrayal and heartbreak on her sister's face. *How did things get so complicated?* she thought to herself.

As she went to Olivia's room, she found her on the floor, sobbing over an old photo album. In the album were photos of the two of them and all the things they had done together over the years... birthday parties, family vacations, paintball wars, dances, learning to ride their bikes, and so much more. They had been so close, and now it felt like they were strangers... yet they were all each other had.

"I'm so sorry, Liv!" said Abigail through tears. "I never meant to hurt you, I swear."

"Why did you have to take him, Abby? He was the only boy I ever loved. It was always so easy for you, but he was the only one who even looked at me."

They continued going through their belongings and reminiscing over the good times, which slowly began to drown out the bad memories.

"Why did you come back for me?" asked Olivia.

"You're my sister. I couldn't leave you down there. I love you." As they embraced, they heard the sound of the moving truck approaching. They looked over to see their parents walk through the door. The looks of pain on their faces were unbearable, but all the twins could do was watch as they packed up box after box.

* * *

As Mrs Manchester walked over to grab the final box, she found the matching set of lockets she had once given to her daughters, one last sign from them that they were watching over her and that they were together again.

My Sweet Emily
Chris Ruland

Emily sat at her desk with her eyes fixed on the window across the lobby, watching with indifference as cars rolled in and out of the parking lot. Her legs were crossed, and she tapped her toe rhythmically on the floor. Her thoughts were as idle as they were on any other day.

Most of the visitors were regulars. Some were homeless. The regulars all knew her face, but none knew her name. Except for one- Guilford Brown. He was a kind old man, though most of the library staff thought him "creepy." He smelled funny, so they said, and his left eye was clouded over with a haze after years of untreated glaucoma. He walked with a limp and carried a canvas satchel that looked older than he was.

Emily blinked out of her malaise when he said, "Hello, Emily."

She saw him standing at the counter smiling. Grinning back, she said, "Sign in, please."

"How's my girlfriend?"

Emily held a sheet of paper over her face as she giggled. "Just started my second semester of college."

"Are you enjoying it?"

"Yes, I am!"

"Well, keep up the work. College is worth it. I could have taken it for free, but I decided not to. Biggest mistake of my life." He smiled again and moved on to the lab.

"What is wrong with that man?" came Arlene's voice. Emily startled and whipped around.

"I didn't see you there-"

"I'd say that old geezer has a crush on you."

"Probably. But that's okay. I think he's sweet."

"He's creepy. I wouldn't talk to him so much if I were you."

Emily didn't care for what Arlene, nor anyone else thought. She pressed her glasses up her nose as she watched Guilford stroll into the computer lab.

"I'm sure he's fine," she said. "After all, what could a sweet old man like that possibly do?"

"You haven't lived long enough to know yet, girlfriend." Emily watched as Guilford found an empty desk and sat at the computer. "What do you think he does here every day, anyway?"

Emily shrugged, and stared out the window.

* * *

The day progressed and Emily nearly fell asleep at her desk when she heard Arlene shrieking from inside of the computer lab.

"Ewe!" she shouted. "What is that? Get it out of here!" Emily stood and looked to the lab and saw Guilford flinging his satchel around his shoulder before turning and walking her way.

"See you tomorrow, Emily," he said, smiling again.

FLASH FICTION ADDICTION

Arlene followed him. "Don't bring that in here ever again," she said. After he had left through the glass doors Arlene turned to Emily. "Cockroaches. Disgusting cockroaches! They crawled out of his bag!" She made a squirming motion like she had bugs crawling on her as she left the reception area.

*   *   *

Guilford shuffled to the door of his apartment and fumbled with his keys. He stabbed at the keyhole a couple of times before finding the correct one. As the door squeaked open he meandered in, allowing light from the hallway to spill into the apartment as he found and tugged at the pull string on the single light bulb, and it flickered on as he turned and shut the door.

He was about to drop his satchel on the table when a hiss dragged from the far corner. "Oh, my sweet girl," he said as he slipped off his shoes. He padded across the single room to the dark corner where a door was fastened to the floor, and he knelt down and pulled at the handle. The door hinges creaked as it opened and the hissing grew louder. A tongue slithered up and out of the darkness and an arm leathered with scaly flesh and spear-like claws protruding from each of its digits reached upward. "My sweet, sweet girl. I've brought you some supper."

Guilford reached into his satchel and drew out several squirming cockroaches. He tilted his hand and they fell into the pit as a slimy tail flicked out of the blackness and a soft growl rumbled beneath. The juicy sound of munching came out of the pit, and the hissing faded.

"Do you like them, sweet girl?" said Guilford. He hesitated, looking down with a caring furrow of his eyebrows. "I know you are very tired of the roaches. But soon, my sweet girl, you'll taste human meat. Yes, I'll feed you with the flesh of the one I've named you after. Very soon, my sweet Emily."

Bank
S. Lyle Lunt

Little Monkey's hungry, but when I ask Mama can we get some food, she just leans harder over the driving wheel. When he starts to cry she reaches into the glove box and throws a Snickers into the back seat. It hits Little Monkey in the face, but he don't cry because he's happy he got a Snickers.

Mama don't tell us where we're going but I figure it out when we pull up in front of the yellow brick building. It says 'Bank'.

Mama turns around. She's been scratching her bug bites and one on her chin is bleeding. "Y'all stay in this car. You hear? Don't get out for nothing. I'll be right back."

She grabs my book bag, the one she told me to find right before we left. "It ain't a school day, Mama," I told her, but she didn't care. She goes into the bank.

Little Monkey has some chocolate drool sliding down his chin. "Mama's getting money so we can get away from Chad." Little Monkey don't answer.

A lady runs out the bank, shouting to a different lady in the silver car next to ours, "There's a bank robbery going on!" and I get scared. Robbers have guns and Mama's all me and Little Monkey got.

"Stay in the car!" I yell. Little Monkey's eyebrows get close together, but I climb out the back seat and run into the bank without any more thinking. The bank doors are heavy.

Inside I see two ladies laying on the floor like they're taking a nap, but neither of them's Mama, because they're fat and have short hair. Then I see Mama hunched over on the floor with her yellow hair covering her face and her hands up like on T.V. and a man has a gun pointed at her. My book bag is on the floor.

I run to Mama. My foot hits a gun and it spins around in a circle. The bad guy has a label on his pocket next to his blue tie. "Get out of here, kid," he says. "Now!"

"Brent," Mama says, "I told you to stay in the car!"

I'm not gonna let some robber kill Mama and leave me and Little Monkey alone with Chad. Chad don't give a shit about us. So I pick the gun off the floor and I point it at the bad guy. His nose holes go open and closed.

"Hey, now, young man," he says, but I don't let him say nothing more. I hit him right where that label used to be, because now it's just a spot of red. The bad guy makes one sigh and then falls straight backwards to the floor. One of them fat ladies screams.

Mama jumps up and grabs my book bag in one hand and my arm with her other hand and we haul ass out of the bank, fast I guess in case the bad guy ain't really dead. Sometimes they come back to life and grab your ankle.

FLASH FICTION ADDICTION

Mama gets in the front and I get in the back next to Little Monkey. She backs up her tires so fast they squeal, and I hear sirens.

Mama turns a corner and screams, "Why didn't you stay in the car like I told you!"

"I had to save you, Mama."

"Where's the gun?" I look down and there it is, still in my hand. "Give it here!"

I climb up on the seat and toss it over. It falls next to my book bag on the floor. The zipper don't always stay zipped and now it's busting out worse than ever because so much money is stuffed inside it. Looks like we're rich.

"Mama, how come Little Monkey's hungry all the time if we had so much money in the bank?" but Mama don't answer, she just keeps whining like Mr John's pit when he got hit by a truck.

"Mama, will I get a award for killing the bad guy?"

"Shut up, Brent! Just shut the fuck up and let me think!"

I shut the fuck up so Mama can think. Behind us I hear the sirens. I let Little Monkey lay his head on my shoulder, and I look out the window and wonder which one's it gonna be, a medal or a trophy, and if when I get it I'll be on TV.

Thankful

J. M. Ames

I'm thankful I haven't lost my mind.

This obese woman, with the fatally aromatic halitosis, is screeching in my face about the price being off by a bank breaking fifty cents. Her vile spittle mists my glasses. The vapid lady behind her is on her smartphone, chattering a thousand miles an hour in some foreign language. Her snot-nosed brat pilfers candy from the shelf, putting half eaten chocolates back before grabbing more to stuff in his face. The snakish line of mindless sheeple is reminiscent of the cars jockeying for gas back in the seventies. Today we are to express thanks for our loved ones and our cherished possessions, but these lobotomized lemmings practically eviscerate each other to get the latest, shiniest must-haves at a slightly reduced price. It isn't Friday quite yet, but the Blackness is already here.

From within my swollen abdomen a vibrating gurgle resonates loud enough to pause Dragonbreath's incessant prattling. Maybe I ate too much at dinner, or maybe the capitalistic consumerism on display is just that sickening.

"Price check on six," I mumble into the malodorous microphone. A groan rumbles down the line, and some of the herd migrates to another check stand. The World's Best Mother frowns at Dragonbreath and I without slowing her frantic diatribe.

Twelve bucks an hour isn't worth this soul-rending torture.

I gasp and grip my side as a sharp pain stabs through me. Cold sweat slicks my forehead, and sudden nausea dizzies me.

Are there furious little dwarves with Lilliputian pickaxes desperately trying to escape my intestines? Dammit, I told Ma the turkey was too pink!

I pull it together and plaster a mannequin smile on my face. The forecast for tonight just got much shittier.

"What's taking so long?" Dragonbreath bellows.

The stench of decay that puffs from her face dissolves what little control I have left. With a sudden violent convulsion, vomit shoots from my mouth and onto Dragonbreath's ample bosom and overpriced, high calorie coffee drink. I mumble a vague apology and bolt for the breakroom, on an unstoppable mission to empty my gullet of the offending poison.

A balding, middle-aged man with an absurdly large moustache pops up, like a game of Whack-A-Mole.

"Excuse me, sir; Can you—"

"No." I shove him out of my way and into the collection of shopping carts that nobody has bothered to line up.

I slam open the smudged, grey door with the Employees Only sign and make a dash for the men's room. My foot catches on a chair leg—because really, who can be bothered to push in their damned chair?—and I crash to the ground, hard. My face cracks against the tile and I try to shriek in pain, but my lungs fail me because the fall has knocked the wind out of them. I lift my head to see a jagged chunk of tooth lying in a puddle of my own gore. The tip of my tongue confirms that the other half is still attached.

"Adam! I just heard you barfed all over a customer and shoved another into a shopping cart. Is this true?" Alison is not a forgiving manager. Probably not even human.

"Yeah, but look, I—"

"I don't need to look. You're fired!"

And then I puke again, some of it splashing onto Allison's ivory stilettoes.

"Ugh, clean out your locker and get out!"

At least there is freedom...

I'm thankful that I haven't lost my mind... *yet*.

Civil Rights
Lael Braday

Lulu stopped by the dog shelter on her way home from work.

"Hey Calvin."

"Hey Lulu. Here for your monthly treat?"

"Oh, yes!"

The smell of the dogs filled her with anticipation of the upcoming delight as she followed Calvin to the rear of the passageway, the end of the line for dogs at this shelter.

A tail-wagging, slurpy creature of indeterminate brown lurched at her, but Calvin held his leash taut.

"Down, Jasper," Calvin admonished.

"Why do you always call them by name?" Lulu asked. "It's so disturbing."

"It's not his fault he's run out of time. Here, take him."

"You couldn't, you know, prepare him for me?"

"You know the law. This is as prepared as it gets. Take it or leave it, sister."

"I hate preparing them. It's so gross." She grimaced.

"5... 4... 3...2 ..."

"Okay, Okay. Can you at least put him in the back of my car?"

"You are the most squeamish zombie I know." He grinned.

* * *

Harvey sat on her front stoop.

"You're always early on treat night. Excited?" she asked him. He smiled and grabbed the leash.

An hour later, after hosing down the abattoir of a dining room, and each other, they inspected the room for errant parts.

He informed her, "Here's a bit of your ear."

"Thanks. I'll get the supplies." Harvey carefully stitched her ear together.

"Ugh, the same ear twice. Does it look much smaller now?"

"No, darling, you look perfect, as always."

* * *

Cuddling in bed on treat night was a luxury.

Wincing at the huge canvas facing the bed, Harvey inquired, "Must we have your ancestor overlooking our love-making? Won't you ever take it down?"

"Never. She's my great-great-great-grandmother. If it weren't for her, we wouldn't be here."

"I know, I know, the first zombie activist. She's the reason we have forty thousand laws governing us."

"She's the reason we are no longer living in caves, eating roadkill to survive."

"Ah, yes. We get to treat ourselves monthly with cast-off, would-be pets."

"Yes! And, we get to purchase blood and offal at the butcher like civilised zombies."

"You're right. I just wish it didn't hang over the bed."

"I wish you could stay the night." She pouted.

"Love, it's just too dangerous."

"I know. I don't want to wake up with you eating my liver, or me eating your heart out. That picture is a reminder that we still have limitations. By the way, I have her skirt."

"The one in the painting? You never told me that."

"It stills smells deliciously of blood. Though I feel a bit guilty, since it's her blood."

"You're a bad girl." Harvey leaned over, puckering up.

She laughed and rolled on top of him.

Tales of a Teapot
C. H. Williams

There it sat listening to their conversations. No one had ever thought to cover its ears as no one knew how to find them. It held a thousand stories, had calmed countless woes, halted the bitterness from their worst arguments and refreshed and revitalised those in need.

Its pastel pink pattern complimented a well placed doily. The silver fracture on its lid showed that even with the utmost care, nothing shall ever remain perfect.

If it could talk—or like the kettle—if it could sing, it would tell of the many lives lived, from high up on a shelf, cabinet-bound, and of days spent moving from tray to table and back again.

Cracked and broken, knocked over by the tail of an excited golden retriever, it spilled its tea, but never its secrets.

Once Upon a Witching Hour
Nick Morrison

As much as the princess hated to admit it, her late stepmother had crafted a clever out-clause. Evidently the late queen had been more than just a cold-hearted, dark magic practicing, vain, old thing. Her foresight was to be commended, even if begrudgingly.

From her tower bedroom, the princess—now queen—stared out at the distant lights of the village. Warm, summer wind whipped wild ebony hair around her beautiful face.

Sleep had descended over the castle and all throughout the fairest land that she ruled. Behind her, the handsome prince—now the king—slept. He had cares; he had worries. Yet he slept, and slept long and soundly.

For her, however, sleep was not only impossible, it was fast becoming a distant memory.

At first she had thought that it was an after-effect of her long slumber. The little men from the forest hadn't told her how long she'd slept in that glass coffin, but the changes wrought in the kingdom since she'd first bitten into that blood-red apple had been answer enough.

Months and months of being under the darkness of an enchanted, deathlike slumber had done something to her mind.

Therefore, it made perfect sense that she would be sleepless for a while after her curse had lifted.

That had been a full season ago. Now she knew better.

She'd done everything to put herself sleep. From making love to her husband—which drained him more than her—to herbs and draughts, to walks in the moonlight around the ramparts. She'd even taken to sneaking into the armoury and practicing with the heavy, steel weapons that the knights used, thinking that physical exhaustion would finally help her succumb to slumber.

But nothing had worked. Not even spells taken from her stepmother's tomes of the arcane had done the trick.

The princess sighed, a pitiful sound on the wings of the warm wind. Really, the night was quite peaceful. The worst of the sleepless nights were behind her now—the fear of not being able to fall asleep had gripped her some weeks after all the initial remedies had been tried and proven failures.

Those nights had been the worst of it, when wakefulness had gripped her eyelids in sharp talons and forced them open no matter what she did. Tears had proven useless, as had prayer and magic.

She greeted the sleeplessness as an old friend now.

As hard as it could be on nights when her thoughts, dormant in the daytime, chose to run rampant through her brain, the insomnia was proving to be to her benefit.

These nights, she could stay up until the sunrise with her beloved king. When they weren't making love, they shared nights like this, when they would speak for hours and hours and learn about one another like a proper man and wife. Indeed, her love for him, once made almost entirely of gratitude and a girlish awe, had blossomed like a flower due to her eternal wakefulness.

Other inhabitants of the castle, those whose job it was to avoid sleep, had become like friends to her now. She knew them, by sight and sound—knew their life stories and their hopes and dreams.

Some nights she would avoid people altogether, and wander through the gardens under the eye of the watchful moon. She'd come to view the moths that fluttered through the night air and the crickets that sang their mating songs as beautiful things, not just pests of the night.

In the witching hour, time was almost an endless thing. She could go to the ancient library of the castle and read from all the books and learn about her kingdom and other kingdoms like her. She could learn about other princesses in similar peril and how their own handsome princes had saved them.

A mournful church bell tolled from the church, three booming echoes on the hour.

A smile graced her blood-red lips.

The cost for breaking her curse wasn't as dooming as her wretched stepmother had hoped.

For though the price she paid for true love's kiss waking her from eternal sleep was to never sleep again, the night was not the end of life or love or learning.

Not if one knew what to do with all that additional time.

New Shoes
R.L.M. Cooper

I look out the window and see little tow-headed Jimmy down the street. He has a new bicycle. Very shiny and nice. He's been riding it up and down the street all morning. I sigh as I watch my Jalen bounce his old patched basketball on the sidewalk and then onto the street. He turns, leaps, and sinks the ball with a clang through the chains. He stops and watches Jimmy ride by and then bends down and carefully brushes the dust from his sneakers. My heart soars. Jimmy has a new bicycle. But my boy has new shoes.

Prehistoric Connections
A. J. Lawdring

One day, a couple years back, I was cleaning out my junk drawer when I found an old telephone. I was tempted to throw the old phone in the trash but I couldn't make myself do it. I love old things. New things make my ass hurt. When it comes to gadgets, I'm never the first one to run out and buy the newest thing on the shelf. Especially when it comes to phones.

Back in 1994, three years *after* they hit the shelves, I bought this thing called a bag-phone. You could plug it into the cigarette lighter in your car and call anyone from wherever you happened to be. I admit; it was pretty cool.

Then they came out with cell phones, and after the kind of peer pressure my mother warned me about when I was a teenager, I succumbed and went out and got myself one of those. It was big and bulky and I was always losing it. I was used to a phone with a cord. In the old days, if you couldn't find the phone you could always walk over to where it was plugged into the wall and follow the cord back to where the receiver was. Or on the handheld models, you could hit the *find* button. I was well acquainted with the *find* button. But cell phones didn't have cords or *find* buttons. The elimination of those features immediately put me at a disadvantage when it came to finding the *gosh darn* phone.

FLASH FICTION ADDICTION

Then they came out with a smaller style cell phone. I'm sure it was so I could lose it much more easily than the bigger cell phone I had before. This new phone was called a flip phone. But I got used to the flip phone, and after about seventeen years, I knew what would happen when I pushed *most* of the buttons.

But in cell phone years, my flip phone had become what the people at the cell phone store called a *dinosaur*. By the time I went in to exchange my flip phone for a newer model that would work with the current networks versus my old analogue network, the manager called all of the employees over to where I was standing. I carefully placed the *dinosaur* on the counter. One young girl jumped back, having never seen anything like it.

"Now I want you all to pay attention," the manager said. "You hook up an old cell phone like this to a converter, and then you hook that converter to this converter and this converter to this other converter and then you can download all of this lady's saved information, and *then* you reverse everything so you can load her saved information into her new phone."

Everyone leaned in, even the young girl who had jumped back. They were paying very close attention. Some lights flashed and I saw smoke coming out of one of the wires on the last converter. The manager got this puzzled look on his face. Then it became a look of horror. He turned to me and said, "Oh my gosh, ma'am, I am so sorry. We just lost all of the names and numbers you had stored on your phone for the last seventeen years!"

"What names and numbers?" I said. Apparently, in seventeen years, I really *hadn't* learned what all the buttons on my cell phone were for.

Mariposa
Michael Allen Roche

Suddenly, I awoke from a deep sleep, clearly remembering the vivid details of the dream I had just lived.

My godmother, Granny, one of my favourite people on Earth, had just died. This was the beginning of the dream, but it was a pleasant dream, not a nightmare, and not sad.

While I was saddened to learn—in the dream—that she was no longer with me in this life, I was happy to know that she would be where she planned to be for the next part of her journey.

As the dream continued, I remembered the fantastic stories she related to me throughout my life. Due to these stories, many folks in the family had come to call her 'eccentric.' Others said 'crazy.' Many people were fascinated by her tales. I believed every word.

She claimed to know more about the afterlife than most individuals who currently walk the Earth. She once explained to me that upon her death she knew—with no uncertainty—that she would be transformed.

When I was young, she had explained the metamorphosis of a caterpillar becoming a beautiful butterfly. According to Granny, she had actually been born as a beautiful shiny new butterfly, nearly ninety five years ago. Over her lifetime, she enjoyed her beauty and grace as such a colourful magnificent creature.

She explained that she would become sluggish over time and her hair and skin would lose its lustre. She would be slow and dull as a caterpillar. At some point, Granny knew she would experience her own metamorphosis again. She told me not to be sad upon her death, as she would be returning to the world as a bright new butterfly.

*   *   *

Soon after waking and recalling the details of my vivid dream, I received a call from my father, telling me that Granny had passed away overnight. I was not surprised. I was not sad. I know she transformed. As I hung up the cell phone, thinking about her journey, and how I would not see her anymore, I received a text message from my brother:

GREAT NEWS! Maria delivered a healthy baby girl an hour ago, 8 pounds, 2 ounces, 21 inches. We named her Mariposa. It means butterfly.

Emily
Donise Sheppard

Emily's white dress billows behind her as she makes her way to the mantle. Her brown hair is in perfect ringlets, pinned to the back of her head. She frowns at the wedding announcement of Mr Thomas Dunlap to Miss Pullin on Saturday, the thirty first of May, nineteen fifty two. She pats her face with powder, but it isn't like she needs it. Her beauty shines through even the darkest soul, so maybe Thomas could be a good husband for her.

I chuckle as Emily pours herself a shot of vodka. She always said she'd need liquid courage to marry a man. She presses the glass to her lips and tilts her head back, drinking it all at once. All I can do is sigh when she pours herself another shot.

"Emily..." I plead, nearly crying. I know she isn't excited to live this life, but it's what women are born to do.

"I know. You're disappointed. You want me to walk down that aisle and marry Thomas as if you and I were never in love. Tell me. How do I do that? How do I forget the past two years?" Her breath catches. She quickly swallows her second shot and pours a third.

"I'm sorry, my love. I wish I could have married you myself, but what life would that have been? We'd have been shunned from the church. Our mothers would die of shame. Two women with a Catholic upbringing don't get married. You must marry Thomas. Your children will have his money and your beauty, and you'll learn to be happy, darling."

Emily wipes away a tear, breaking my already saddened heart. I quickly rush forward, wanting to hold the woman I've hurt more than anything. I stop, just a foot away, and reach out as she downs her third shot, slamming the glass on the mantle. The door bursts open, and our mothers enter, eyes only for the bride.

"Where is your veil, dear? Why aren't you dressed yet?"

Emily takes a deep breath as her mother pins the veil in her hair, taking care not to mess the curls.

"You're absolutely stunning," my mother tells her, tears in her eyes. "Laura would have loved to be here for you."

I smile at Mother. It's been months, and her heart is almost healed. She has finally stopped crying. Emily nods and hugs her, thanking her for coming on her special day.

Emily's eyes glisten as she walks down the aisle. "I love you," she whispers so only I can hear, before walking up the stairs to greet the groom she doesn't care for.

*   *   *

"I want Laura, dammit!" Emily cries, clinging to the bed rails for support.

I wipe tears from my eyes as I rush into the delivery room. "It's alright, Sweetie. You can do this."

"Emily, we need you to breathe and push."

"I can't!" she cries, sweat dripping off her face, crying harder.

"You can!" I urge.

She pushes, screaming out in pain.

"Stop pushing!"

"There's so much blood!"

The nurses and midwife frantically try to help, but their voices are drowned out by Emily's screaming. I kiss her forehead and cry as she lets out a blood curdling scream.

There's a flash of bright light and Emily's screaming suddenly stops. Her head rests on the pillow, eyes wide and glossy, mouth open.

One of the nurses rush to her side and confirms her death. She lost too much blood.

There is a small cry, and I turn to see her beautiful daughter. The midwife gently cleans her before handing her over to the other nurse to care for while she tends to Emily.

I turn back to the light and smile at my Emily, who has finally joined me. Oh, how I wish she wouldn't have had to suffer first.

"Laura!" she cries, running to me. "Why are you still here? It's been years!"

"I've been with you since the accident. I'm here because you were still crying for me." I hug her, enjoying the smell of flowers in her hair, before a tug begins to pull me to the light. "I have to go now. I hope you'll join me when your children are done crying for you."

"I only just got you back."

"But you can't grieve when you're dead. No one is left to mourn for me. I'll see you soon, my love."

I kiss her gently before walking to my fate, pausing for one last look at my angel before welcoming my new life.

Anonymous

Umair Mirxa

Balthazar had never really been attracted to redheads, especially ones with fair skin. Given the choice, he preferred raven hair and olive complexions. The woman who sat before him now, however, was the exception to every rule.

The first he'd known of her approach was a hint of berries in the air. *Odd.* He didn't expect such pleasures in the pigsty he'd chosen for his watering hole tonight. Still, he'd known life to be stranger.

"Buy a girl a drink?" she said, casually taking the seat next to him. The perfume of her skin was intoxicating.

"Eh, why me?" he said. "Wha'll ye have?" *I'll risk it.*

"I'll let you know," she leaned in, drawing his eyes, "in a moment. First, I'll have your name."

Her voice spoke to him of love and warmth and happiness. Embraced him so as never to let go. Caressed, oh, ever so gently, the flames of his desire.

"Balt. Ye can call me Balt," he said, wrenching his eyes up to look into her own.

There, he found new treasures, buried deep and shining bright. *She could finish a man with those eyes.* The strain he felt in his breeches told him he wasn't wrong. Spellbound, he traced her features with his eyes. He could almost taste her lips as they curled up into a smile.

"Short for Balthazar, no doubt," she said. "And that is what I shall call you. It is proper."

"Call me wh'ever ye want, luv. Wha's a lass like ye doin' in a shite-full dump as 'ere, anyho?" *Why is she here? Could it be a trap?*

"Oh, the same as you, I suppose. A girl wants to quench her thirst. Days like these, there are few places she can go."

"Wha's yer name then?" he asked. "An' ye still ha'e nuffin' te drink. Oi, barkeep!"

"Hush. I shall have one presently. Let me, for the moment, simply enjoy the pleasures of your company."

She crossed her legs, and Balthazar let his eyes wander. From the toe of her boot, riding up the hem of her dress to her waist, and exploring the abundant delights on offer around her neckline. She was voluptuous in ways no woman had any right to be, and the dress clung to every perfect curve in all the manners a man can commit sin.

"Ye haen't even given me yer name," he said. *I'm bored, now.*

"What, pray tell, would you do with one, were it given?"

"Why, cherish it, 'course. Use it, for te remember ye."

"My, aren't you the most charming of devils. And you would wish to remember me?"

"'Course!" *I remember them all.*

"Even if I were to stand, and leave right now?"

"Look 'ere, lady. It's jus' yer name. Give it or don't."

"Ah, but it isn't, is it? Mama always said be careful who you give your name. They have power, see? Names do."

"Pfft! Le' me a'least buy ye tha' drink." *I think I like her.*

"Oh, don't huff! It ill becomes you. In any case, what does it really matter? Call me Aurora for the dawn. Would it change how you think of me? Think of the prettiest name you know. Remember me by it. Aphrodite, maybe?"

"I'm ou'ta 'ere, if teasin' me all ye's about," said Balthazar, dropping a few coins onto the bar.

"You did promise me a drink. I think I'll have it now. Not here, though."

He offered his arm, and led her out into the street. She directed him into an alley a ways down. *Enough of these games already.*

He pinned her up against a wall, and sank his fangs into her neck. The taste of her, the scent of berries mixed with blood, the feel of her body pressed against his own—together, they made him almost careless. Almost.

She had neither screamed nor resisted. He was too good a hunter to allow it. Softly though, she now moaned, sinking into his trance.

"Cassandra," she whispered. "My name's Cassandra. Will you remember me?"

Balthazar smiled. At last, he could control her. Compel her to his will. He decided to keep her—for a while, at least.

"Of course, I will," he said, holding her up as she fainted against him. "I remember them all, darling."

She was right. Names did have power. Her cohorts could wait at the end of the alley all night. He gathered her up in his arms, and vanished into the night. *Alexandra would like a taste. She loved redheads.*

FLASH FICTION ADDICTION

Cranes
David M. Donachie

Tuesday, 28th September—a grey and windswept pre-dawn, punctuated with the tap-tap of single raindrops against the windows. I rise at 5:30 am; wash, dress, and eat toast by six, then put on walking boots, a waterproof coat, and a pair of 7x40 binoculars, before heading out into the tenuous morning light. Sunrise is at ten minutes past seven.

A flock of seven cranes have gathered near a construction site in the lee of Tod hill, just short of the high street. Roosting, they have crowded close, so that their white metal jibs are in danger of colliding. Single red lights blink sleepily on the top of each one.

There is already traffic on the road nearby: trundling buses half full with returning shift workers, impatient suit-wearers hurrying through the darkness in search of early trains, a whirling gutter-cleaning machine; but I cut off into a sidestreet of uncollected wheelie bins and closed backdoors, and secure an observation spot where I can rest my elbows on the top of a telephone junction box and watch the cranes without disturbing them.

I focus my lenses on the two biggest, who are standing with their jibs touching—just the lightest of contacts—the sign of a mated pair. And yes! Hiding between them, only just visible through the latticework of their legs, a single offspring! A tiny luffing jib, barely twenty metres high, with a bright shiny cabin and three blinking lights. Even as I watch, it swings its jib from one side to the other, looking up at its protective parents with what I imagine to be love, or more plausibly hunger.

The presence of a breeding pair, albeit with a half grown child, suggests that this group might be an extended family. The larger cranes towards the outside edge—a towering straight-jib type with a concrete ballast, two forty five metre self-builders with unlit signs on their sides, and a single unadorned luffer standing on its own—might be bachelor relations. Then again, it was just as possible that they were unrelated comrades, or even rivals, looking to disassemble one of the mated pair and take its place! Sadly, I've seen such things before.

Out east the sun is rising over the water, flooding the decks of the cargo ships with washed out light. There are cranes down on the docks, ancient squat-backed patriarchs that I may go look at later, but for now, I keep my binoculars trained on the flock of seven, knowing that this is the moment.

In less than a minute the first rays of sunlight have caught the top mast and winch assemblies of the largest crane, the straight-jib that I'd identified before. The red warning light blinks out, so for a moment it looks like the crane is dead. A moment later the crane is gone, fleeing back across the city to wherever the dawn should find it. The other cranes follow all in a rush—a brief murmuration of thrumming cables and whirring winches—scattering to their building sites.

The family group lingers for a few moments longer, letting the sun paint them with light. The adults tap jibs, then drop their hooks, so that the youngster is embraced—for a moment—between the swinging cables. Then the right-hand adult and the child are gone, leaving just the single crane behind, towering over the building site.

I hang around a little longer, letting the sounds of the city wash over me. Soon the first early workers are arriving at the building site, unchaining the gates and heading sleepily for the kettle in the Portakabin office, hardly sparing a glance for the tower crane soaring high above their heads, waiting patiently for dusk and its returning family.

Winter

Aditya Deshmukh

Sometimes I still feel the silky touch of her long auburn hair brushing against my chest, and hear her carefree laughter as she kisses me.

I run upstairs and peer through the half open door. She is lying on bed, awake, but barely so, staring at the crib with longing eyes.

I knock. She doesn't hear. I walk to her and sit beside her. She doesn't notice.

"He's gone, honey," I whisper as my eyes turn glassy. "Our baby is gone."

She looks at me. Her gaze is warm no longer. It's distant, lifeless and cold, so cold, just like winter.

Fool on the Hill
Pam Van Allen

"Ten thousand ways to die, a hundred billion ways to live," the Master intoned.

I gazed into the inscrutable face of my master, expecting more. He stared back for a moment, evaluating me. Then his expression softened into the eyes-half-shut, demi-smile he so often wore.

"I don't understand."

"You may not understand for many lifetimes."

"I hope one day I understand your riddles."

"*Out of nowhere, the mind comes forth.* You will understand the day you stop trying. Leave me now, and choose one of the hundred billion ways to live."

I had pretzeled my legs into the lotus position in an effort to impress my master. One leg was prickly with pins and needles—my punishment for being so idiotic. He could see right through me.

I hobbled into the monastery's dining room.

* * *

The kitchen served the last meal at ten forty five in the morning. Obedient monks didn't eat after eleven. I claimed my bowl of rice and fastidiously ate each grain with chopsticks, meditating between nibbles on the bounty as I had been taught. We ate one grain at a time to remember how the Buddha had subsisted on only one grain of rice a day.

Butsu sat opposite me with his bowl of rice. We never spoke at meals, so I didn't acknowledge his presence or look at him when he arrived. He was running late for final meal and would be hard pressed to finish before eleven, one grain at a time. I knew I had a long way ahead of me on my journey, because his Zen name always made me laugh in my mind, although it wasn't funny. Butsu was Japanese for Buddha.

In my peripheral vision, I caught Butsu stuffing a wad of rice into his mouth, then another. A wave of judgement about his behaviour rose in me.

Butsu finished his rice before me and left the table, washing his bowl in the long sink at the end of the room. He dried it and stacked it neatly with the others. The gong sounded for eleven. I looked regretfully at the five grains of rice I hadn't eaten. This was what Master meant by deciding how I would live. Did I eat after eleven or waste food—a moral dilemma. I chose to waste the food and bussed my bowl as Butsu had done.

Wash the dish to wash the dish, not to get it clean.

I contemplated Master's injunction—choose a way to live. Hadn't I already done so? Six months ago, I chose to be a Zen Buddhist monk in this remote monastery on a hill. I sought to cleanse my soul, to seek enlightenment, to strive for exit from the wheel of reincarnation, and to work for the enlightenment of the world. I left my home and family and withdrew here.

Now I rose before dawn, cleared my mind for meditation several times a day, worked our humble farm, and laboured in the kitchen. I avoided the nearby village where the people consider the monks odd. I dedicated my life to the Dharma and took refuge in the Buddha.

I noticed how often the word *I* drifted through my mind. One intention of Zen practice is ego death. With prolonged meditation practice, consciousness ceases to reflect upon itself. The meditator experiences it as a *letting go* and feels as if he or she is falling into the void. It is almost like being wiped out of existence. As long as my mind was full of *I-me-mine*, I wasn't likely to achieve ego death.

The voice of the master echoed in my mind. *If you meet the Buddha on the road, kill him.*

*   *   *

After evening meditation, I wandered by the fountain in the garden. I imagined drowning my ego in its trickling waters. Motionless, I sat watching the sun sink below the horizon. The spinning of the Earth created the illusion of the sunset.

Daruma, a fellow neophyte, settled on the bench across from me.

"How many ways are there to live?" I asked.

"The way you have chosen, and everyone else's."

"What way have you chosen?"

"Eat, sleep, meditate, study the Dharma. What else is there for us who have taken refuge and hope for release from the Wheel?"

"Have you heard the sound of one hand clapping?"

"No, have you?"

"I have failed. Master thinks I'm a fool."

"Is that a bad thing?"

"Maybe not. I'll only know when I no longer am one."

Horses for Courses
Alan I'Anson

"Hey there! You look like a gambling sort. Come over here. I have something that's right up your alley!"

Old Arthur raised his eyebrows. A gambling sort? Okay, the hands deep in his pockets might be grasping a few betting slips, but this market trader couldn't know that.

He wandered over and cast an eye over the stall, which appeared to hold nothing more than trashy, second-hand goods and brickerbrack.

"Not much here," he remarked.

The stall-holder tapped the side of his beaky nose. "I don't put this out for just anyone. I only show discerning gentlemen, such as your good self!"

Arthur chuckled at the traders gab.

"You want to see?"

"Go on then, "Arthur agreed. "You twisted my arm."

"Not at all," the trader said, and from under the stall he brought out a round chromed object, flat on the bottom, with a little rectangular window in the top. It looked like nothing much, but it caught Arthur's curiosity.

"This little device," the trader said with a flourish, "will tell you the winner of every horse race."

Horse racing! That was his tipple. But it was ridiculous, and Arthur told him so.

"I guarantee it works," the stallholder said.

"Guarantee?"

"Yes indeed. If you don't like it, you can bring it back for a full refund. No questions asked."

Arthur scoffed, but it had such a lovely shine to it. He could use it as a paperweight if nothing else.

"How much?"

"To you, sir, just one pound."

"One pound? That's cheap."

"You drive a hard bargain, sir."

"But I didn't—"

"Do we have a deal?"

Arthur looked at the shiny globe and smiled. "I'd say we do."

He placed an equally shiny pound coin on the table, and the stallholder slid the chrome ball to him.

Arthur turned it over in his hands. "So how does it work?"

"Ah yes," said the stallholder with a knowing wink. "Turn it upside down and name race time and the course. Turn it the right way up, and the name of the winning horse appears right in the little window."

Arthur laughed. "Before it's even run?"

"Try it."

FLASH FICTION ADDICTION

Arthur laughed again, but this time something in the man's eyes dried the humour in this throat. He checked his watch, turned over the ball and said, "The 12:45 at Newbury." When he turned it back over it was showing a name in the little window—Johnny's Jape. He remembered it was in the race because it was the rank outsider. How could this little *toy* even know that Johnny's Jape was in the race, let alone if it would win?

"The 12:45 at Newbury?" The stallholder angled an old style radio at Arthur and switched it on. "Let's listen in, shall we?"

The race had just begun, and though it seemed like Arthur's horse was going to win, it fell at the last hurdle, and Johnny's Jape went on to victory.

Arthur looked at the chrome ball in amazement. "And it will do this for any race?"

The stallholder nodded and grinned, his teeth kind of big and yellow and crooked.

Had they been like that a moment ago?

"You take it and win a *fortune* with it." His tongue slipped out and moistened his wormy lips.

Yes he could! He could rush home, grab next week's rent and put it all on the winner! But what was the point of that? When Dorothy was alive, he used to pore over the races and call out the names to see if she liked any of them. He used to love hearing her comments.

Ooo, Johnny's Jape, I used to date a guy called Johnny.

He still enjoyed his daily flutter on the horses, checking the form and placing his bets. If he had this thing, he'd lose that pleasure.

"I've changed my mind," Arthur told the stallholder. "I want my money back."

"You do?"

He plonked the ball down on the table. "Come on, give me back my pound."

The stallholder reached into his bag and handed over a pound coin, his face dark, his teeth almost brown and overlapping.

Arthur accepted it, his hand trembling, and quickly walked away. When he glanced back, the stallholder was still watching him, his mouth set in an ugly sneer.

Then he brightened, his smile instantly back, and beckoned to someone in the crowd.

"Hey you there. You look like a gambling sort. Come take a look at this. It's right up your alley."

Cinnamon
Daniel Newton

Nutmeg. Or Cinnamon.

Jona felt the panic start to rise again. He closed his watering eyes and drew another agonisingly slow, stinging breath through one semi-functional nostril. Controlled, gentle inhales only, so as not to compromise this last lifeline by demanding too much of it and causing it to constrict or block further. The thin beads of cold air teased his starving lungs. Maintaining a viable airway is always of prime concern for anyone waking to find himself wrist bound and tape-gagged with a freshly broken nose. Still, Agent Jona Leonardi registered the familiar smell through the sack he was in. Cinnamon perhaps. Or something else. Cardamom?

The UPSILON infiltration had gone well. Leonardi had achieved excellent penetration during his insertion within the notoriously slippery Czech mafia, not only returning critical fresh intel about what, and who, were behind this recent spike in transnational activity, but also multiple new leads into the broader European network. There were the predictable rackets of small arms and military merchandise, and of course the Holy Trinity of drug trafficking: heroin, amphetamines, and cannabis. These things weren't of primary interest to Jona, however. They could keep the guns and dope, and Borders could handle that anyway.

The chief objective of this investigation was now Leonardi's strategic positioning within the intercontinental human trafficking scheme he'd uncovered, just as his SIS operations team had suspected. Awkwardly, what no one had foreseen was the double-cross by his partner. Ferguson, the old bastard.

Gaining his breath and his composure, Jona quickly realised he was very cold and something sharp was binding his wrists behind his back. Ferguson, or whoever had done this, hadn't bothered to blindfold him, which right now seemed a small mercy given that his visibility was limited to the inside of a canvas cocoon. Doubtless, the sack was secured from without. And there was noise. An engine. A very big engine. He was on an aeroplane.

With a shimmy of his shoulders, Jona confirmed by learned feel that the tactical shoulder holster under his jacket had been stripped. No gun, no clips, and no blade. His bound hands discovered they had left only his leather wallet in his back trouser pocket. Drawing it out as carefully as his numbed fingers would manage, he felt it was empty, except for one card. That wasn't good. Jona knew it would be his identification and, fake as it was, he also knew that someone was waiting at the end of this flight with instructions to collect this bag and quietly dispatch the incapacitated 'Tomas Kozlow' within it.

Behind his back, Jona worked at the little zipper on the coin pocket of his wallet, eventually wrenching the tiny zip tab free of its slider. Rolling further onto his side, he found the inside seam of the bag with his hands and set to work with his makeshift thread picker.

The cargo hold of the aircraft was vast and well lit. Metal shelving ran the length of both sides of the space with most of the broad central avenue occupied by camouflage netting wrapped pallets and large trolleys loaded with canvas bags. Bags just like the one with the orange 'Z' sprayed on it that Agent Leonardi had occupied minutes earlier, and that now lay at his feet. Jonah busted the plastic cable tie binding his wrists on a nearby fire extinguisher bracket and finally tore the silver tape from his mouth, breathing deeply of the chilly air.

Definitely cinnamon. And cardamom. No, cloves.

Jona let out a low whistle as he began inspecting the payload. The pallets were military care packages—an immense inventory of pharmaceuticals and medical supplies, radio and computer equipment, diesel generators and machining tools. There were freshly laundered uniforms in a digital camo of tan and muted greens. And there were weapons: Rack after rack of freshly minted AK-12 Kalashnikovs and PYa handguns, and whole pallets of ammunition crates. The sacks were mail bags addressed for the Russian territory of Kaliningrad and filled with letters from home, as well as gifts of family photographs, good luck trinkets, and even parcels of baked goods.

*   *   *

Agent Leonardi completed the final stitch and pinned the surgical needle back into the seam. Holster restocked and a loaded AK-12 at his side, Jona reclined into a comfortable position within his sack. He almost pitied the poor souls tasked with collecting this particular delivery. Settling in for the remainder of his transit, he smiled to himself and quietly opened a wax-paper bag of homemade cinnamon tea cakes.

An Empty Christmas
Nerisha Kemraj

Alistair knew no one would come and yet a little glimpse of hope niggled at his insides—Nana's faith. Surely, the holidays brought forgiveness and cheer. He smiled at the glowing tree that Bonnie kindly decorated just the way Nana used to. The warm Christmas lights brought him some comfort and he felt Nana's presence stronger, as always during this time of the year. Bonnie insisted on staying with him after noting the mountain of mail she took to the post office the week before, they were returned unopened. But he would hear none of it—she deserved the time off to spend with loved ones just as he would have liked to.

He glanced now at the printed invites that went unanswered. Nobody took the time to read them. Maybe they had moved. Or it got lost. Deep down the truth rang clearly. Kids never forget, they say... They were wrong. His forgot him.

Nana always said, "Don't be so hard on them, Dear, they need love. It wouldn't hurt to show them you care."

"What they need is for you to stop babying them," he retorted, ignoring the hurt in her eyes.

What he wouldn't give to bring those moments back now—to show her he cared, to show her he understood. And to show his kids a bit of love instead of the harshness he threw their way.

Being a military officer didn't mean he should run his house the way he did his soldiers. The repercussions of his actions surfaced now—a lonely life of his own doing.

Resigning to weariness, the fight in him dissolved like the whiskey accompanying him. He tucked his napkin into his shirt and his meal took him back to the days with his sweetheart. The aroma from the scrumptious chicken roast wafted through the room leaving him salivating. Thankfully Bonnie grasped Nana's exact recipe to the tee. And apple pie crumble for dessert, his favourite... slowly he removed the packet he concealed from Bonnie, looking around to make sure it went unseen, he added on the final ingredient of his demise.

As his throat constricted in reaction to the nuts, with blurry eyes he saw Nana waiting, hands outstretched. She called out to him and he surrendered, ready to embrace his endless rest. As long as it was with her—everything seemed easier then.

Together at last.

Desire, Duty, Deed
Kain S. Bishop

The window has a western exposure; the sunset explodes through the frosted panes with a kaleidoscope of pastels and angel's arcs. Bathed in splendour; my study becomes animate. The hunter green wallpaper and dark teak wainscoting shake off their sober demeanour and find amusement in humiliating sophistication.

I put aside my work when the sunset comes, for my paw will forget its intent, and rather, begin drawing lazy shapes across the parchment in India ink. In anticipation I have poured myself a stiff draught of heavy cream and then study the paintings of my Tom and Grand Tom adorning my walls. Sometimes, I even talk to them as I sip; with one ear twitched towards the window and an occasional glance in the direction of my bejewelled portal to the world outside.

I have had long conversations into the night with these portraits; the advice from beyond the grave always sensible and sober. My arguments are less sound; my heart aches to be caterwauling and singing. The alleys call me to roam and hunt... but we are beings of distinction, felines of refinement; and our duty comes before all things.

Of course when it is desire that destroys duty, this determines deed. For she often stops in front of my window for a casual bath; her tongue caressing her shoulder and paw before grooming her face and ears. This goes on for maybe half a minute. She never once looks in my direction. And then she is gone. Until tomorrow. So I go back to work, my heart ever anticipating.

So often a moth to her flame. But in the words of my Tom: "Remember, Son, the moth ends up burning away."

Cleaning Out the Closet
Traci Mullins

If he'd known he'd have to tell someone someday, he never would have done it. He'd been keeping the dirty deed hidden on a shelf in the back closet of his psyche for years, and he was determined that it would stay there.

But they told him that if he wanted to stay sober, he'd have to take stock of what was on the shelves, like taking inventory of cans of mouldy fruit or rancid Spaghettios. The problem was, he had a super sized can bursting with twenty year old shit. No one could possibly have on their shelves what he had on his.

When the hour came to come clean, he held his nose as he pulled out the stinking stock in trade. He kept his eyes fixed on the ground until he heard his sponsor laugh.

"Oh, buddy, I had a dozen cans of that!"

Ashes to Ashes
Rita Kruger

I know there is a nervous breakdown somewhere in my near future. I can feel it lurking in the darkness that surrounds me. It circles me like a hyena, waiting for me to show a sign of weakness before he will pounce. This divorce is cutting me into a million pieces, and the carnivores are gathering for the feast.

I built up a storeroom filled with the correct phrases: this is for the best; this will make me stronger; I will look back at this as a building block, not a stumbling stone. They all sound equally empty spoken in an insomnia haze.

One night, three months into the ordeal, I scrutinize myself in the bathroom mirror. I hardly recognise the woman looking back at me. My eyes drift across the strange planes of her face. Her mouth tries to smile at me but something horrible happens to her face and it ends up a disaster. Deep furrows cut into the skin and muscle on her forehead. She looks ten years older than her real age.

They say that the eyes are the windows to the soul. When I look into her eyes, I hear a deep satisfied growl from the darkness. Despite all the pretence, I can see her fear; I can smell it like the aroma rising from a million cups of coffee. I can feel her uncertainty pulse like a vein and the taste of her naked pain is like bitter blood on my tongue.

She closes her eyes, as if she can somehow bury her pain, hiding it from my scrutinizing stare. I force her to open them again. Her defences crumble, showing the true depth of her pain.

Ashes to ashes, dust to dust. My vision is blurred by the tears in her eyes.

Revelling in the Storm
Martina Speranza

As the sea disappeared, swallowed by a dark haze at the horizon, he thought *Here it comes.*

Only seconds before, the vast expanse of water glimmered of thousands of shades of blue and green, the sun danced through its waves and kissed the pearlescent foam that trimmed them. Now the sea was turning grey. Only a few strokes of a dark green glided under the agitated surface.

A distant roar slowly began to rise; at first just a light sigh, then an *uuuuuhh* resonating through his bones; and then a furious, terrible cry that crossed the horizons in every direction, filling the world and lacerating the sky. Low clouds came, cramming from everywhere to form a dark shroud which deceiving softness delighted him. Lightning moved under their dark skin, menacing yellows and blinding greens that fell into the water and on the ground, scourging everything they touched with their glaring fingers.

He raised his head in an offering to the fury of the elements, when the rain finally poured from the sky. Needles stung and bit him, carried on the wings of the wind to pound on the earth, on the sea, on his own body.

FLASH FICTION ADDICTION

The rain flew alongside the ground, and his heart flew with it.

The trees bowed their heads, surrendering to the vehemence of the wind and the merciless strikes of the rain. Sharp drops hit his eyes, bouncing furiously on his light body. He felt his own foreign thoughts come and go like waves, now clear, now distant and remote. He would find Her, join Her at last. Forever.

His heart sang with the storm.

One by one his companions withdrew, hungry and shivering, abandoning the sea and their activities to seek refuge where the cold strong wind and the rain and the fierce waves would not find them.

He didn't notice, and they didn't call for him; the Storm was his, and they knew. The females looked at him, mournful, maybe hoping his gaze would find them, but he didn't see—or didn't want to.

His heart was a drum in his chest, his beating echoing the blasts of thunders, threatening to tear up his flesh to gush out where She was. The wait, the endless torment between Her appearances, the constant bite of an hunger that couldn't be satisfied and a thirst that could not be quenched, the bittersweet pain; it all vanished drop by drop, washed away by the rain and blown out by the wind.

He could feel his body find new life, vibrant of desire and strength. The hunger that had woken him at dawn rapidly receded, the sleep that still obfuscated his eyes dissolved. He started looking for Her, not with his eyes, but with that precious shard that he knew instinctively they all – rock, animal and sprout – nurtured in the centre of their beings.

Only one of his companions still remained by his side, trembling unnerved by the frenzy that emanated from him. *Don't go*, he told him. *Don't go, you won't come back.*

He didn't answer. He flexed his body instead, offering himself to the Storm, preparing to reach Her and made Her his own. He felt the roar of Her voice answering and deafening him, Her wind enshrouding him wildly and tear him from the pleading voice of his loyal friend. *Not now,* he thought. *Not now... but soon.* Wanting to give in to the rising urge, resisting because it was necessary.

What he was waiting for appeared at last, lighting the sky with a sombre glare. The sea revolted against the storm, its waves writhed in vortexes and lashes, throwing themselves against the dark, sharp rocks seeking death only to find new life.

He heard Her voice calling for him. It made his bones rattle and his skin go numb. His heart exploded in his throat and his mind went out in a burning white flash.

At the height of the Storm and his own vigour, he threw himself into Her arms, pushing his body through with fury. His companion tried to follow, but could only resist a few seconds by his side: it was not him that She wanted. He bid his friend farewell with a sorrowful cry. He didn't hear and didn't see him falling back.

FLASH FICTION ADDICTION

The seagull rose in the air, once again defying the wind that twisted and tear, headed toward the pulsing heart of the Storm.

Meaningless Coincidence
Nileena Sunil

I've always had an affinity for bookstores.

Right from my childhood, I would find myself searching for bookstores in every street. I would take refuge in them whenever I fought with my siblings or friends. I could spend hours in the bookstores, browsing books. As a child, I never had the money to buy books, so I did my best to ignore the store-manager's glare as I walked away without buying anything after spending hours there. However, that was not going to happen today. Today, I was at the bookstore with a purpose.

I went to the counter, and asked the man behind it-a hefty giant of a man-if he had *The Ominous Trial* in the store. He told me he had never heard of the book. I sighed. It was the thirteenth bookstore I had visited looking for the book.

I realized I should have had expected it. Everyone in my country had heard of *The Ominous Trial* after the events of June 8, 1971. However, it was wrong of me to assume it would be that way all around the world. I returned to my hotel room, my heart heavy with the understanding that I would not know the ending of the story for quite some time.

I supposed there was a certain irony in the fact that I was unable to read the book written by my Aunt Tilly, who was my closest relative while growing up. She was a sweet old woman, and the fact that she wrote a book about a gruesome murder-a book which is said to have inspired an even more gruesome murder-seemed bizarre. I suppose that everyone, even the ones closest to us have hidden depths we are unaware of.

Aunt Tilly became a recluse after ever the incident. She shut herself completely away from the outside world. I didn't think she even knew that the murderer had escaped-thank goodness for that! She had always been such a model of piety. I couldn't begin to imagine the guilt that haunted her.

I thought it was unfair that she had to feel guilty-and that people made her feel that way. The book was found in the murderer's bag. That didn't have to mean anything. It was foolish to assume that the murderer was inspired by it, when it could have just as easily been meaningless coincidence.

My motives for the murder definitely had nothing to do with the book I was reading. I didn't even know that the book my aunt wrote had anything to do with a murder. She was so keen on keeping the plot of the book secret. Yet, after the murder, they insisted on making a connection with the book they found in my bag.

I was never able to finish the book, and I am now dying to know the ending. Of course, there would be many more bookstores where I could search for it, but I doubted I would find it in this country. I didn't think I'd ever be able to return to my own country. I would have to quell my desire to know how it ends as I faced life every day.

A New Day
J.W. Garrett

Shielding my eyes, I stepped outside, even though I wanted to fade into the woodwork of our New Orleans townhome. Day one at a new school yet midyear for everyone else. Dread filled me.

Moving was hell. Eighth grade was bad enough but here—worse. A stench penetrated the air, and I glanced in disgust at the canal in the middle of the street. *Isn't it against the law to have an open cesspool in a neighbourhood?*

In the distance, I heard the low hum of the school bus approaching. It ground to a halt, and I quickly found an empty seat, scooted to the window and gazed outside. *Maybe no one will notice me.* Minutes later my bubble burst.

"Move over, ugly."

I turned and opened my mouth to speak.

"Yeah, you, shut up." She smashed me into the side of the bus with a hearty laugh.

I attempted to move. Her size and weight prevented that. *Didn't anyone see or hear what was happening?* My gaze travelled to others in a silent plea for help. A third joined us in the seat, jamming me tighter against the metal and glass of the bus. I waited anxiously for the ride to end, my cheek glued to the window, unable to take in a full breath.

When the bus lurched to a stop, she shoved hard against me, then stood, saying, "I'll see *you* later." Her grin exposed crooked yellow teeth.

I cringed then finally took a deep breath. *How can I get back on this stupid bus?*

I meandered through the halls, moving like an automaton from class to class, paying no attention to anything but my impending ride home with my accoster. I found the office; I felt an *illness* coming on.

* * *

"I'm sorry you didn't feel well, dear. A day's rest will do you good."

"Yeah, maybe." I threw a shoe at a roach inching up the wall.

"So many disgusting bugs here." My mother shivered. "Did you get it?"

"I don't think so." I grabbed a dictionary and followed the creature, releasing the book over its creepy form, covering my ears, anticipating a crunch. "Dead," I said, stomping on the book in affirmation.

* * *

FLASH FICTION ADDICTION

Day two. I wiped sweat from my hands as I waited for the bus. My breath came in short gasps. *Maybe I'll hyperventilate and pass out before the bus arrives... Nope, here it comes.*

I picked my seat, watching as others loaded. I spotted her smirk; she headed for me. Her expression changed when someone behind her grabbed her shoulders and pulled her backward.

"You, sit!" the other girl said to my attacker, throwing her into an empty seat. "Leave her alone, bitch."

"I'm Kathy," she said, joining me in the seat. "It's okay. She's in my crew. I got you."

Dumbfounded, I sighed and beamed with gratitude. Now protected, and my life forever changed, the transformation began. *Her crew? Hell yeah!* I was hers. Time for a real education.

Innocence is overrated.

Home Again
Stephanie Ayers

I sit in my rocking chair enveloped in darkness. A small slit of sunlight shimmers on the cold linoleum beneath my feet. If I listen hard enough, I can hear them calling my name.

* * *

"Lucy, are you ready to go?" my mother said, her blondeness a slim shadow on the far wall I was desperate to ignore.

"Lucy?" she called again, temper peppering her voice. I didn't care. All I wanted was to sit here wallowing in sullen misery in the dark. She never let me just be. I'm not like her, all peppy and perky and social.

No, I'm about as anti-social as they come, more by choice than anything else. I could have friends if I wanted them, but having friends was too much work. It required plastering on fake smiles and exchanging insincere pleasantries I could do without.

My mom didn't understand this, though, and tried to force me into activities that were neither interesting nor fun. I wasn't graced with athletic skills. Roller skating caused me pain. Church youth groups were too chipper. Sporting events held in too bright

FLASH FICTION ADDICTION

gymnasiums that smelled eternally like sauerkraut and wet dog made me retch. The darkness under the bleachers gave way to illegal activities I wanted no part in.

No, I'm rather content just being me. I do my greatest thinking alone. I'm at my best when I'm alone. People like me? We're a dying breed. The rest of the world doesn't get us. They think we need fixing or something. Solitude does not equal broken.

The last time she took me to a sporting event she discovered the brutal lines carved on my arms. They were a mixture of red and pink, old and new, evidence of my fascination with self-inflicted pain. There's something about the merlot coloured liquid weeping from white flesh that arouses me. Of course, she didn't understand that either.

My mom finally had enough. She made an appointment with some quack who rented a corner office in the building where she worked. After spending a mere fifteen silent minutes with me, he questioned my mother's capabilities in providing for me. Their shouts echoed through the empty hallway. My mom shut the door to his office so hard as she left it made the doorknob rattle. I'd never seen her so alive. When it was all said and done though, she eventually surrendered me to his trust.

"Lucy!" Her voice was red hot now. I stared at her shadow for a minute more before acknowledging her. She softened and sighed.

"I don't know what else to do with you. You've wandered so far away, I fear you'll never find your way home again."

*   *   *

I sit in my rocking chair enveloped in darkness. A small slit of sunlight shimmers on the cold linoleum beneath my feet. The fancy white shade is pulled almost all the way down the way I like it, revealing only a small portion of my entombed reality. The gold field beyond the wired window fades away into the rolling green hills edging the horizon, enticing me. If I listen hard enough, I can hear them calling my name.

Seven Breaths
Susan Reabuck

She woke up in a cold sweat and immediately reached for her gun. She scanned the dark dirty room and saw nothing out of place. The chair was still firmly wedged under the door to the hallway. The windows were still boarded up. She focused on slowing her breathing. If there was a threat she needed to centre herself. She couldn't afford to waste bullets.

The air in the room was sweltering. She would have killed for a fan right now. Ha, there were plenty to be had, just nowhere to plug them in.

One breath. She felt the sweat run down between her breasts.

Two breaths. She heard the cockroaches scuffling on the floor.

Three breaths. There is a noise in the tiny attached bathroom. She raised the 9mm slowly and aimed.

Four breaths. The light came on startling her. Her aim never faltered.

Five breaths. The toilet flushed. The door opened.

"Hey, babe. What's up? I didn't mean to wake you. Just needed to piss."

Six breaths. She closed her eyes and counted to four. He wasn't real. He was gone. She had put him down the second time herself. She held him when he took his last breath and then stabbed him through the eye when he woke again.

Seven breaths. She opened her eyes and he was still there. Naked. Walking towards her. Her fingers gripped the trigger. One slight squeeze and it would go off.

"Babe, come on. Put it away and lay with me. You've got to be tired."

He sat on the bed and she felt it move under his weight.

She felt his hand slide across her belly. She felt his lips nuzzle under her ear. She took a sharp intake of breath. His hand was warm against her sweat soaked skin. She knew this wasn't real. She knew.

Slowly she lowered the gun and placed it carefully on the bedside table. She heard the roaches scurry away. He gently pushed her to the bed and she let him. She let him taste her and feast on her. It felt unbelievable. She stifled her cries with the mouldy pillow, even if it wasn't real she couldn't afford to make too much noise. He entered her and she grabbed hold of him. He felt so real. The familiar muscles in his back. His broad shoulders. She dug her nails in and he hissed and took her harder. Yes, she missed this. Them. The climax took her off guard and she cried out into the night. She could hear something scurry away at the sound. Even the small animals knew it was dangerous.

FLASH FICTION ADDICTION

When they were both spent he lay next to her and kissed her neck, breasts, and ravished her lips. She curled up and lay her head on his chest. He wrapped his arm around her and pulled her close. Even in the heat he felt good. Safe. Real. He ran his hand over her hair.

"Sleep princess. You are safe now. I am right here."

She allowed her eyes to drift closed. She felt the single tear fall down her cheek. There was none of this anymore and she knew that.

* * *

She woke up in a cold sweat and immediately reached for her gun. She scanned the dark dirty room and saw nothing out of place. The chair was still firmly wedged under the door to the hallway. The windows were still boarded up. She focused on slowing her breathing. If there was a threat she needed to centre herself. She couldn't afford to waste bullets.

The air in the room was sweltering. She would have killed for a fan right now. Ha, there were plenty to be had, just nowhere to plug them in.

One breath. She felt the sweat run down between her breasts.

Two breaths. The banging started on the door. Then the moaning. She heard the cockroaches skittering to safety.

Three breaths. The door broke and she could see them. Too many. She looked at the boarded windows. She would never get out.

Four breaths. She went to the bathroom and peered out the small window. There were hundreds of them.

Five breaths. The door crashed in. She raised and fired. She would not go down without a fight.

Six breaths. She felt her flesh tearing. It hurt for a few moments and then stopped.

Seven breaths...

The Riddle
Susan Gibbons

"There's something you should know, in case I don't come back." Gretchen blinked back tears as she looked across the booth at her twelve-year-old daughter, Lindsey.

"Come back from where?"

Gretchen ignored her daughter's question. "You like riddles, don't you, Linds? There are thirty-six monkeys at the zoo. Each have only nine toes. How many toes are missing?"

"It sounds like a math problem. I don't like math."

Gretchen forced a laugh.

Lindsey grabbed a crayon from the cup on the table and wrote on her paper placemat. "Nine toes."

"Remember the numbers in order."

Lindsey scribbled out the nine. "Thirty six monkeys have nine toes. Thirty-six times nine, That's two hundred. No, wait. Add the five. That's three hundred and twenty four."

Gretchen shook her head. "You're supposed to find out how many toes are *missing*. You found out how many toes the monkey *have*."

"You tricked me!"

"That's what riddles do. You have to pay attention to how it's worded."

"The answer's thirty six because each monkey is missing one toe."

"Exactly."

That was the last time Lindsey saw her mom, but the riddle stayed with her.

"Thirty-six monkeys with nine toes. How many toes are missing?" she mumbled. "Thirty six toes are missing. You never came back, Mom!" She tried not to hate her own mother, but it was hard. Especially today of all days—her twenty first birthday.

Her doorbell buzzed.

"Lindsey Simmons? Sign here, please." The mailman handed her a package. She figured her grandparents had sent her a present as she sliced through the tape to open the box. Inside, she found a book of riddles and an envelope. Written on the envelope was *Remember your numbers in order*. She shoved the package across the table in horror. It fell to the floor with a loud thud. She snatched the book from the floor and turned to page thirty-six. Nothing. She turned to page nine. Again, nothing. She slammed the book on the table.

"What the hell am I doing?" Lindsey cried.

Inside the envelope was a Greyhound ticket for that day and a handwritten note, *I hope you're not too angry to come visit me on your birthday.*

Curiosity got the better of her. She stuffed the book and some clothes into a bookbag and took an Uber to the station.

"Gate thirty six. bus nine," the attendant said.

"What?" Lindsey blinked.
"Gate thirty six, bus nine."
"Where does it go?"
The man looked at her ticket again. "Portsmouth."
"Portsmouth?"
"Yes, ma'am, about a two hour trip."
"I don't know anyone in Portsmouth."
"Maybe the ticket master gave you the wrong ticket. You can go back up to the wind—"
"That's okay. I'm on an adventure today to solve a riddle."
The attendant tipped his hat. "Have a great day!"

During the ride, Lindsey scanned through her new book, not able to concentrate on the riddles. She wondered what the next part of her mom's riddle meant. Thirty six. Gate thirty six. Nine. Bus nine. Thirty six? When she was younger, she paid careful attention when the numbers crossed her path. She secretly hoped it was a combination to a train station locker that held a million dollars, like she saw in movies.

"Portsmouth!" The bus driver called out.

Lindsey gathered her things and stepped off the bus. She searched for anything with thirty-six on it. Discouraged, she walked across the road to a bench where a man with a baby sat.

"Waiting for the next bus, too?"

Lindsey shrugged.

"Ah, must be your first time. It won't be here for another hour. It comes at ten and two today. There's a little hole-in-the-wall place with decent food around the corner, if you're hungry."

"Is that the only bus that comes here?"

"Here, yes. The bus to go out of town picks up across from the restaurant. Who you visitin'?"

"Someone I haven't seen in years."

"Ah. I understand. It's hard, ain't it?"

Lindsey, freaked out by the man, said, "You know, I think I'll go get something to eat. Around that corner?" Lindsey pointed to the left.

The eatery was congested with people. Lindsey sat on the only open stool at the counter.

"Sorry, it's visitin' day," a waitress apologized.

"Visiting day?"

"At the Women's Correctional Institute. Most are either waitin' on bus thirty six to take them up there or they just got back."

Lindsey took in a deep breath. "Yes. Sorry. Thank you." Thirty six, nine, thirty six. Her mother was telling her how to find her all these years.

Cindy

Louise O'Neill

Cindy slammed the ruby lipstick onto her dressing table and peered in the mirror. Picture perfect, despite the uncontrollable feelings welling inside her. Her mascara hadn't run and a smile was plastered on her face, as usual.

Lately, she was finding it increasingly irritating being unable to show her true feelings. Cindy picked up the green eye shadow and applied it liberally. Her unblinking eyes bored into the mirror, trying to carve her wilful thoughts into it.

But it was no use. There may be a fire of jealousy and rage burning inside her, but the prosthetic image staring back reflected no illusion of this. Forever a victim to her false smile.

Glancing towards the lipstick again, fond memories danced through her head when Lily would apply her make-up for her. They would pretend they were princess sisters and spend hours dressing up in different outfits together. Cindy's smile was real then. How she wished she could go back to those times when it was just the two of them.

These days Lily barely acknowledged her. Cindy couldn't remember the last time Lily had made her pretty by doing her hair and make-up and dressing her up in gorgeous outfits.

Lily had a new friend now who she did all that stuff with. With that thought, Cindy's burning inside was relit. She felt she was going to explode from the inside out. Her face should have been the colour of the ruby lipstick. But it remained the peach colour of her foundation.

Cindy wandered over to her wardrobe and opened it up, displaying her numerous outfits. Her eyes rested on a red velvet ball gown, adorned with a V shaped cluster of silver diamonds on the neck area. It was fit for a real princess.

She could hear the boom boom of Lily's footsteps, so she placed the dress on her bed and sat next to it. Maybe, just maybe, she thought.

The door opened. Cindy gazed into Lily's eyes as Lily made her way over to her.

"The dress is perfect," said Lily, when she found it. "Fit for a real princess." Lily felt the fabric and marvelled as she placed the dress up against Cindy, beaming.

Cindy's insides fluttered.

Cindy could feel the familiar pangs of excitement as Lily leaned over Cindy's castle and started rummaging for the make-up box. But when Lily reappeared it wasn't the silver metal box she clutched.

Cindy's soul interlocked with her enemy's. Her rival's eyes, free to move as they pleased, glinted, bewitched by the dress. Cindy could see snow-white teeth peeping out from a bemused smile. She shed a tearless tear as her antagonist winked at her whilst Lily played dress up with Barbie.

A Man's Heart

Suanne Kim

Whatever your mother may have told you, the best way to a man's heart isn't always through his stomach. His cock will often suffice quite nicely.

That's the situation I currently find myself in: hounded by a man who refuses to let me go because I give good sex.

Rowan is hot. Dimpled cheeks, fiery red hair, and a firm physique that would have any woman salivating.

What a waste of a specimen.

His personality and lifestyle are incompatible with mine and have proven unworthy of my talents. He's boring. His idea of a good time is cuddling on the sofa while watching TV then having vanilla sex for dessert. I crave excitement, variety. I prefer to go out and party. After a year of being in a committed relationship, I've come to feel stifled.

One night, I try to convince him I'm switching teams.

"Pfft. You're about as lesbian as I am. I know what you're trying to do, Callie. You're just scared. You've only had one night stands. But we belong together."

When I threaten to file a restraining order, he calls my bluff.

"Stop fooling around. I've never been abusive—verbally or physically. Would you really have me arrested and ruin my career for loving you? You're not that kind of person."

He's right. In my heart, I don't have it in me to destroy a decent man just for being clingy and begging for affection. By that standard, we'd have to incarcerate children.

Children.

That gives me an idea. If there is one thing I know about Rowan, he doesn't want kids. He disdains them almost as much as I do.

A week later, I litter my apartment with literature about adoption and invite him over. He picks up a brochure from Goodwill Adoption Services. "What's this?"

"I've been doing a lot of soul searching. I want kids. It's time. I may have to start off as a foster mom."

"Are you crazy?"

This is the response I had hoped for.

"How many are you talking about?"

I think of a number and settle on, "Boatloads. As many as I can. I want to make a difference in children's lives."

Crossing his arms, he challenges me. "Get real. How would you support them all?" He shakes his head. "No. We should adopt one. Maybe two, if you feel that strongly about it. But we should get married first. Adoption agencies prefer couples."

We? Married? Oh, dear God. How did an attempt to break up solicit a proposal? It's time to bust out the big guns.

"Rowan, it's not just that. I have something I need to show you." I fish out a box of albums from the back of my closet and hand it to him.

The albums are numbered and document my life, one that starts in Cambodia, living in squalor, and ends with a move to the US, becoming a career woman, as well as my myriad of other transformations through the process.

"This is you? You were...?"

"A man. A boy. Once upon a time."

His eyes dart between me and an old photograph of me on the boys' soccer team. Shock registers as he scrutinizes my features. "But you look so..."

I shrug. "We, Asians, tend to be more petite. It's easier for us to make the transition."

Rowan grows quiet, sullen.

"I've been trying to explain. We're not right for each other. I didn't mean to lie or hurt you. I'm sorry. I really am."

It appears my new strategy is working. He remains silent although I can read the range of emotions on his face from betrayal to loss. Now his complexion burns a bright red which indicates he's furious.

"Do you think I'm that closed-minded? That shallow? You think I'd leave you because you weren't born a woman? Hell, maybe because you were once a man, you know exactly what I like. You're beautiful—inside and out. I love you for who you are. Don't you understand?"

Flabbergasted, now I'm the one who's lost for words.

Maybe I've had it all wrong. Maybe I move on to new people because I fear they will discover and judge the old me.

And maybe, just maybe, the way to a man's heart is truly through...his heart.

The Living with It
Mike Callaghan

Ella cursed the blades of rain that lashed at her face. Bitter cold pierced her cheap overcoat. Worn boots squelched in the mud. Her toes were fast losing feeling. But she found solace in the numbness. She'd need it.

Ella hated everything that was about to happen, but desperation led to dark places and she was backed firmly into a corner piled high with pig shit. If she wanted to climb out again this was the surest, dirtiest, bet. There'd just be the living with it.

A wretched figure emerged at the top of the hill, leaning into the gale, battling their way towards her. Aidan. The only person she knew who was in it deeper than her.

"You came?" he sputtered as he drew closer.

"You knew I would."

Aidan drew back his hood a little to reveal his searching, needy eyes. The boy Ella had once loved had long gone.

"I knew you had to."

Ella spat dismissively. "Aye."

There was no point regretting the things that had brought her here. It was done. Holden was in the dirt now. There was just Aidan. But get this done now and she could make the break.

"Listen to me, Ella, listen. The deal, Northwood's deal, is real. He's giving us another chance. We can get clear of this."

"Aidan, you can't trust him," Ella heard herself say. She didn't know why, it was far too late. They weren't young lovers any more, they weren't even friends. But the instinct hadn't gone. Not yet.

"You got a better way? You were always the smart one."

Ella couldn't hold his accusing glare.

"It's our last chance, Ella! We need to do this. Just keep your mouth shut and do as I say."

Aidan stalked away, still expecting her to follow his lead.

"What's he offering?"

"Enough," Aidan replied.

Ella remembered Aidan's mother back in Dalrec, all the worse off for having a son out in the world. Would he make that right given the opportunity?

"Let's go then," she said.

*   *   *

Ella did as Aidan said and kept her mouth shut. They did their bloody work. She didn't know who the men were, they were just in the way of something she needed, it was that simple. If they found themselves on the sharp ends of her blades, chances were they'd swam in the gutter long enough to put themselves there.

Aidan got what he came for, as Ella knew he would. He wrapped it up tight, away from the rain, and they left nothing but bodies behind. Making their way back along the sodden forest path to Northwood, a lightness returned to Aidan. He laughed freely, a burden lifting from him, a glimmer in sight. But not from Ella. It wasn't done.

* * *

By the time they made it to Dounne, Aidan's old arrogance was creeping back in. Self-assurance beamed from him as he presented the package to Northwood. He had done everything that had been asked of him, it was time for the rewards. Northwood, for his part, was nothing but amused by Aidan's swagger, and grinned back at him through 'bacco stained teeth and matted beard. The older man seemed well pleased with what Aidan had delivered. In return, he placed a large bag of coins onto the table.

Aidan was still smiling when Ella plunged the knife into his chest. His joy quickly gave way to disbelief as he sank to his knees. Northwood rose from his stool.

"There's few finer sights than watching hope die in a man's eyes," Northwood chuckled.

Ella watched Aidan all the way as death dragged him down, pulling his soul apart. She let the weight of it hit her. The adrenaline, the pain, the numbness. The betrayal.

When Aidan was finally gone, Northwood threw the money at her feet. Aidan had been right about one thing, there was enough.

"And now you can go," Northwood spat finally, gesturing to the open door.

She could go. But there'd be the living with it.

Room 101
Gregg Cunningham

Bah I've got nothing, an empty head, and a desk full of blank paper. All I do is stare at that damn clock on the wall, and watch as the days tick by. Hell, even Sam and Dean wait patiently for some illuminating flash of heavenly inspiration. Maybe if I sell my soul...no I can't do that again, not after what he made me do for my last publication! I have had to take several lifetimes of showers since, and still the stench of sulphur follows me like a bad smell! No, no more offering my soul, or selling my soul, or whatever it is he wants me to do with my soul. I'm done with that Infernal place of false promises. I'm just going to sit down here on my butt pillow, and force a story out, even if it does flare up my demonic haemorrhoids again. God, the things that guy does with a hot poker. I tell you, that Deity has no sense of originality.

Never, and I repeat...Never, sell your soul just for a story, not even if he promises a best seller. He loads that bloody contract with so much small print, and celestial gobbledygook, you're paying off the 1250% interest rate long after you have paid your lengthy bar tab up. Look at what my last piece cost me, I mean a thousand words and a guaranteed six likes with the option of three shares after a week. Man, I cannot tell you the hurt I had to go through for *that* post.

Going viral! Shit, that contract is gonna set you back the nine concentric circles of suffering, *and* both testicles. Don't believe me? Well just ask Dante. Remember Sodom and Gomorrah? Well that was him on a *good* day. You don't want to mess with that dude, or you'll end up turned to salt, or worse, pushed down that heavenly helter skelter clutching your slide matt and ending up in Room 101, with me. Which isn't really a bad thing considering the alternate to be truthful. All that right hand of god nonsense, meh, boring if you ask me.

And to think he calls *me* the Devil incarnate.

Hey... maybe I could get some poor sucker to sell *their* soul to me? Yeh, why not? There are plenty of schmucks up there who want a story published, plenty of plebs who want to bask in that 'Fifty shades of Glory.'

Hey you! Yeh you...Wanna make a deal?

It'll make you rich, have a think about it, but just don't take too long. Hear that? That's the sound of opportunity knocking-I just need one small favour, nothing much. And I promise you, you'll never even know that the sad pitiful thing is gone. Honest!

"Hello. Yes, do come in, the door is open…"

Younger by the Minute
Gabriella Balcom

It's not October yet, but I think I'll be ready when Halloween rolls around this year. Although I've never been real gung-ho about costumes or dressing-up, I have the perfect disguise now--a type of alter ego. All I have to do is tilt my head forward, then pull it back until it retracts inside the additional flesh which--for incomprehensible reasons--has appeared underneath my chin. I couldn't believe my eyes when I realized a roll had formed there. Lately, it looks as if it's about to give birth to a second—a child of sorts. Oh, I'd make it vanish if I could, but in the meantime, I'm trying to have a better attitude about the whole thing.

My best friend Lila tries not to laugh, but her eyes get all sparkly when she thinks something is funny. Blunt as heck, she asks, "Are you growing a storage compartment under there, Nellie Sue?" Of course, she's a fine one to talk. She's always been chubby, and years ago chubby rolled straight into what the world calls 'obese.' But she's fifty nine years old and counting, and staying in shape gets harder with age.

However, I *never* thought that would happen to me. I'm only forty--well, forty-something--so why do I look like an example of an overstuffed cushion? I've managed to keep my weight average, so to speak. Maybe fifteen to twenty pounds over what's considered optimum, but I noticed the area under my chin changing in recent years. The skin kind of relaxed. Losing its former tautness, it grew slightly loose instead, then droopy. Cushioned. The transformation continued from there, moving from that to what could only be described as a bigger, beer gut type of thing, except it seemed to have gotten lost and ended up near my neck rather than anywhere close to my stomach.

This aging business has been bothering me for a while, and my whole life, I've faithfully followed tradition without question, and added a year to my age on each of my birthdays. Well, I've decided to make a change. From now on, I'm going backwards.

Lila asks what motivated my decision, and I tell her the truth. It's not the chin thing. It isn't the wrinkles I've seen pop up on my body, even though some of them are bigger than I like and could also serve as storage. It isn't even the grey hair, although I admit I was *not* ready to discover my first, much less my tenth... or thirtieth. But I won't go there.

I'm just ready to be younger again. Oh, I'm not burying my proverbial head in the sand as far as my body changing. I mean, I don't think I'd look *that* bad with my butt sticking up in the air; it's not the best part of my anatomy, but it's certainly not the worst. Saying I'm a year younger won't halt further changes or undo what's already happened, but it'll make me feel better.

With my new credo of going backward in time, it won't be all that long until I reach my optimum age. Where will I go from there? I'll just stay that age and be young forever, of course. Where else?

Priorities

Vince Carpini

The Scout dropped out of the saddle, handed the reins to a sentry and crossed the muddy courtyard toward the keep. He turned in his bolt-rifle and sabre and marched up the narrow, winding staircase to the command centre. He saluted the room lazily, accepted a glass of water from a bespectacled analyst and slumped heavily into a chair with four different legs next to a table littered with loosely-organized stacks of paper.

A woman with colonel's stripes and a lattice of volt-bomb scars across her face nodded impassively as a radio operator gestured helplessly at his console.

"Finally," she said, catching sight of the Scout. She handed a sheaf of papers to an aide as she walked over and looked him up and down. "Report."

The Scout held up a finger as he finished the water, then pulled half a cigarette from his breast pocket and lit it with a broken match. The Colonel shifted her weight.

The Scout looked at the glowing tip of the cigarette, then at the Colonel.

"You ever hear of Laika the Space Dog?" He asked. The Colonel blinked. "The Old Russians found her on the street and shot her into space. First animal in orbit. Wasn't much room in the capsule, so they trained her by putting her into smaller and smaller cages for weeks at a time. They made her a tiny space suit and stuffed her into *Sputnik*-2. The Americans called her 'Muttnik,' get it?"

The Colonel frowned. "Report," she said again, more forcefully.

"For a long time folks thought Laika'd been euthanized, or that she'd been left alone up there in the cold and dark until her air ran out. The truth is that the ICBM they strapped her to failed to separate. The sustainer motor kept heating the capsule and Laika was cooked alive.

"Later, they built a statue, immortalized her in bronze – and then the New Bolsheviks melted it down to make swords.

"Before her flight, one of the scientists brought her home to play with his kids. The day of the launch, the techs who sealed her in the capsule kissed her goodbye. They cared about her and they sent her to die anyway. She'd been chosen to perish, and they still showed her love. I think about that a lot."

He took a long drag on the cigarette and blew twin plumes of smoke through his nostrils. The Colonel's eye twitched.

"Anyway, the N-B have overrun Checkpoint Echo. They'll be here in an hour."

A dozen people stopped what they were doing and stared at him in stunned silence. The Colonel's mouth hung open. The aide dropped her papers and began to cry.

The Scout clicked his tongue and dropped his cigarette in the empty glass. "Shit. Should I have started with that part? I should have started with that part."

In the Dark
Mercedes Siler

River closes her eyes and presses her face into her hands against the doorjamb. "One, two, three. No giggling, I can hear you. Four, five, six, seveneightnineten! Here I come."

She activates the flashlight app on her phone and scans the dark room, her belly tickly like a little kid. This would be a lot more fun with more people. She used to play flashlight hide-and-seek when she was in high school. She and her friends would get drunk and run through the woods with their plastic cups, trying not to giggle or scream in terror of the dark and get found out.

"I'm going to find you, little girl."

She grins and starts tiptoeing softly through the dark house, listening for giggles.

She shines her light under the table and the kitchen sink.

"So, you're not hiding in the kitchen?"

Her heart-beat thumps as she creeps through the living room in the dark, the only light the little spot in front of her. She looks behind the big recliner and in the corner between the TV and her mother's old hutch filled with knick-knacks.

"Not in the living room either," she calls out.

She checks the bathroom, and under the bed in her mother's room, then the closet in the little girl's room and under her bed. But she would never hide there. She and the closet monsters were on tentative good terms, especially now that she was treating them to jelly beans for good behaviour—but only *tentative* good terms. And the under-the-bed monsters were a completely different story.

She takes a breath before entering her own room, extra quiet, listening for the rustling in her closet or giggles from under the bed.

Nothing.

Her heart beats faster, desperate to find her now and to not be so alone in the dark. She shines her light under the bed, in the closet. Nothing.

She shines her light around the room and sees her, a folded-up little doll with big beautiful eyes sitting in the corner.

She picks her up, sighing a breath of relief. "I found you."

The little girl wraps her arms around her mother's neck. "Mommy, next time I want to go with you when we play."

"If you came with me, no one would be able to hide or seek."

She wraps her arms around her tighter. "I just want to be with you."

She closes her eyes and squeezes her tight. "Of course, baby girl."

The Minds of Birds
B. Sharpe

"Momma. Wren fly. Wren fly!"

"Oh my God. River!"

I leaned into my heavy steps. Leaves and sticks crunched in protest. My tank top clung to my skin. Sweat creeped through the crevices of my daisy dukes. I fought for breath with the heavy humidity.

Wren, tippy-toed and little hands aflutter, grunt-chirped ahead of me. He somehow dance-picked his way around the non-existent path through the trees.

In the distance, I could hear the rickety, rumbling pickup trucks as they whooshed down country tarmac. Soon, I'd need to snag the thirty-six pounds of Wren before he ran across a busy highway. I thought I had more time.

My thoughts meandered to our old clapboard house about a mile back with its seventies décor. Mom, snug in her bed, after a double shift at the Swamp Fox Bar, where she waitressed and endured sweaty palms and jeers just to get by. Wren, never able to understand, already woke her up once this morning.

I realized I'd lost sight of Wren. I paused. My mouth went dry. I ran in the direction I'd seen him go. Just in time, I caught sight of his brown curls as he passed through two trees in open grass. Open grass- the shoulder, he was on the shoulder of the road! I sprinted.

God, please...

The highway appeared before me as I caught up, empty and quiet. Wren laughed. I turned my head right, saw him in the road, and smiled. Past him, I saw that no cars came from that direction.

Habit made me turn my head left. Pale, white, pristine, *alien*, the white car made no sound, at all. At first it was fifty feet away, before I knew it, forty. How fast was he going? I heard a faint purr.

Oh, my God... Wren. I turned my head again, saw him, directly in the car's path.

I didn't think, I acted. I ran. The car was thirty feet away. Would I make it in time? Now the car was twenty feet away. When I came within ten feet of Wren, I jumped. I sailed. Wren's body slid into my outstretched arms, crashed into my shoulder. We began to fall, not quite clear of the shiny bumper that still came forward. I turned my back to the asphalt as I hugged my little brother to me.

A wall slammed into my foot. *Crunch! Twang!* Immense pain rushed through me as we spun, then slammed to the ground.

A sound, a high-pitched whine filled the air. Blackness crept along the edges of my vision. My chest felt tight. My breath came fast.

Click. I heard the sound, but it didn't register.

A dark-haired man appeared in my line of sight. His mouth moved, but I couldn't hear it over the whine.

I stared at him, unable to move, to speak. I couldn't even think.

An odd contraption, black, appeared. He flipped it open, pressed somethings on it, and put it to his ear. His mouth moved, as if he spoke into it. He looked down at me, his eyebrows drawn. Then he looked at my foot and his hand went to his forehead. Tears rushed down his cheeks.

The whine began to fade. A numbness I hadn't notice before began to withdraw. The pain screamed from my foot. Maybe I screamed, I don't know.

"Hey, hey. Shhh, shhh. Here, let me take him."

Take what? Whatever it is... No, mine.

He kept talking, but I zoned out.

A wail, repetitive, replaced the whine. Then, another wail, some different, joined the first, so that the two seemed to go around and around and chased each other.

Whatever was in my arms was alive and began to squirm. I just stared into oblivion. My arms tightened around the warm bony thing I held to me.

So tiny, so fragile, it felt like I was holding a giant, squirmy bird. Its little bones must be filled with air. My arms were a cage. If I let the bird go, it would fly away. I didn't know why, but I couldn't let it fly away.

I began to feel tired, so very tired. The black edges spread.

The wails came screamed closer until it felt like they were on us. A man appeared over us in a blue uniform, he came closer as if he knelt down. The bird in my arms fought, screamed.

The cop had piercing blue eyes and a Brooklyn cop nose.

The black spread until there was nothing else and I began to try to sleep.

The bird slipped out of my arms. "Momma. Wren fly. Wren fly."

"Oh my God! River!"

The Truth about Fairies
Sheri Velarde

Fairies are real. A little too real if I'm being honest.

Let me go back to how I first discovered fairies, well, my own personal guardian fairy at least. It all started with some belated spring cleaning, when I reached my disused liquor cabinet I heard small hiccups coming from the back of the cupboard. I sat startled for a minute, but then decided I must be hearing things and started removing bottles to be dusted. However when I came to the whiskey in the back, I heard something that I couldn't explain away.

"Let go, bitch," came a small but belligerent voice.

I did indeed let go of the bottle, causing it to shatter and revealing the small winged woman drenched in the liquor who had apparently been hiding behind the bottle. "Way to go you idiot. I was drinking that." The little creature came out, shaking her fist at me.

Shocked, I fell on my butt, just sitting there and rubbing my eyes. "I must be losing it," I mumbled to myself.

Taking no real notice of what I was saying or doing, the small woman like creature just kept cursing at me and complaining about the lost booze. "If I weren't bound to you as a guardian I'd kick your ass for this. The vodka is already so watered down that I can't even get a buzz. Are you going to replace my whiskey or what?"

"What are you?" I finally asked.

"I'm your damn guardian fairy, isn't that obvious. And I'm pissed off. Go get me more liquor or I'm not guarding a damn thing."

"There's no such thing as fairies." I blurted out, which only enraged her more.

"What the hell do you think I am? Are you really this thick? No wondered you were deemed to need a guardian; you're too stupid to make it through life on your own."

That statement somehow shocked me back into myself, being a woman in a man's world meant that I did not take kindly to people questioning my intelligence. "I have two master's degrees, one in mathematics. I may be confused but I am not stupid, that is for sure. How long have you been here in my cupboard? What do you mean by guardian. I'm not giving you anything until I get some answers."

"Fairies are magical creatures. Haven't you ever read anything? We are guardians of certain people and places. Some power radiates from those we are supposed to help, I don't know the specifics. I was drawn to you when you were still a kid. Something to do with your dad I suspect. I've been here helping you get through the rough times. My name is Tiana, by the way." She seemed to have settled down and I could feel that calmness running through me as well.

"You've been with me since I was a kid? Why have you never shown yourself to me? I don't understand any of this."

"Humans rarely understand anything. As for why you haven't seen me before, I didn't think you could handle it. As a child you would have flipped out and as an adult you would think you were imagining things. I thought it better to stay hidden." Tiana shrugged. "To be honest you haven't really needed me in years, yet the power that drew me to you in the first place has not broken, I'm still held here for some reason. I really have been bored these past few years."

"Is that why you were living in my liquor cabinet?"

"A fairy has to spend her time doing something."

"So you hit the bottle? The fairies in literature don't seem like they would turn into drunks."

"Most authors don't know the truth about fairies; our personalities and actions are as varied as humans. Don't be so judgmental. I'm stuck here until you don't need me anymore."

"What do I need you for? You just said I haven't needed you in years. Why are you still here?"

"Hell if I know, only time will tell, but something big must still be on the horizon for you and you are going to need some magic to help you through it."

I sat there, stunned and wondering what this fairy and her prediction that something big might be coming my way. "Where does that leave us?" I asked.

"In need of more whiskey."

A Helpful Friend
K.M. Jenkins

The ground was wet beneath her feet as she crunched through the underbrush. Animals danced along the trees and the forest floor that was music to her ears. As quiet as possible, she snuck deeper into the woods hoping not to get caught. The sense of adventure overpowering her judgement.

Kero didn't think about her father's wrath she would earn for disobeying him. He wanted her to stay near the encampment hoping to keep her out of trouble. Little did he know she was several hundred yards away.

Her dress clung to her ankles as the seams got caked with mud and water. She kept her eyes and ears alert to anyone or anything that could approach. Silence greeted her as Kero's feet climbed over a large fallen tree trunk. She stumbled and braced herself against the muddy ground laughing. Getting dirty was one of her favourite pastimes. Kero got to her feet and cleaned her muddy hands on her dress.

"Father will kill me for that, oh well." She laughed as she advanced on her journey into the woods.

A loud crack was all she remembered as she fell through the ground into the darkness below. Scared eyes looked around trying to figure out what happened. Kero adjusted herself checking for injuries as she heard a soft whimper. Slowly, she stood trying to get a feel for her surroundings as her eyes adjusted fully to the darkness. With her hands groping in the dark she moved towards the source of the sound.

Kero brushed something soft and warm in the darkness. Another whimper filled her ears as she looked down. In the darkness wide brown wolf eyes looked back up at her. She gasped in surprise.

"What are you doing down here?"

Tenderly she embraced the little ball of fur realizing it was only a pup. The little guy favoured his back left leg as she cradled him to her chest.

"Don't worry, I've got you."

Soft whimpering sounds came from the pup as Kero took in her surroundings. "I have to find a way out." Her eyes noticed a soft glow coming from the north side and moved closer. Once in front of the spot she realized there was a large hole she could walk through. Without hesitation she moved forward.

She walked for what seemed like forever with the bundle of fur growing heavier in her arms. Voices filled the tunnel as Kero grew closer to the light. Then finding herself once again in the bright light of the sun she saw Lord Thomas.

"There you are!" he bellowed. "Where did you run off to?"

"Nowhere."

He glared at her when Kero locked eyes on her father. His grim expression told her he wasn't pleased. It was never good to piss off the king. A shuffling of earth and branches caught her attention as she turned to see the whole disappear. *Where did it go?*

"Kerowyné... What do you have there," her father asked with a serious tone.

The pup popped his head out from under her arm and looked about. He seemed to be happy to see the sun again. "Papa, I found a friend. He is injured do you think you can help?"

King Tyler smiled as he got to his feet. He walked over and tenderly took the pup from his daughter and looked the little wolf in the eyes. "I think we can help him."

"Thank you, Papa."

He turned towards the tent then looked over his shoulder at his adventurous daughter. "This doesn't mean you're off the hook for disobeying my order. You weren't supposed to leave the encampment, young lady."

Kero looked down at her feet. "I'm sorry... I got bored."

"Hmmmm..." he replied as he entered the tent. Healer Kent followed him leaving her alone with Lord Thomas.

Lord Thomas looked down at her. "You look a mess. Go get changed and try to stay clean this time."

Without another word she ran off towards her tent. A flash a white caught her eyes. She looked around looking for the source as a white wolf appeared. Worry showed in the wolf's eyes.

"Don't worry, my Pa will take care of him," she whispered.

FLASH FICTION ADDICTION

The wolf disappeared from Kero's sight. As a howl of thanks filled the sky. Smiling to herself Kero walked into her tent to change and go meet her new friend.

Rose
C. L. Steele

Every birthday for thirty-five years, Rose received nothing. She didn't know why she kept expecting different results. A voiced Happy Birthday, quick kiss, sometimes on the lips, and off to work. Maybe this year he'd get her a gift, a card. Something that said I know you. I love you. I appreciate you're alive today.

After decades, this time she couldn't cry. Music didn't change her mood. The car didn't fly fast around curves. In fact, this year the car came to a dead stop in the middle of the two-lane road, no light, no cross-road, no turn—stopped dead. Cars honked, swerving around as she sat in the car looking ahead staring. A bubble built up deep and painful in her stomach. It rose pushing and fighting its way, hitting every ridge of the oesophagus, a twisting knife-like pain. For a moment she thought she'd die on her birthday. Would that make it special? Would he sit at a grave wondering and remembering? Remembering what? All those special times of nothing.

Deep from her soul the words came—fuck. Fuck you.

She'd been fucked out of years of happiness and memories and a sense of mattering. Fucked out of meaning and worth—of being loved. But it wasn't only him who'd fucked her. She'd fucked herself, out of courage, worthiness, love, and memories. She'd allowed it. Rose did a U-turn and drove home.

The garage door rose in a steady grind. She stormed inside, slammed the door shut, threw her purse down.

"Enough," Rose shouted reaching the living room.

He lay on the floor, still.

The bastard had died on her birthday. Realization fell that while she sat in the middle of the street fucking him, fucking herself, he was fucking dying. She couldn't even let him die in her arms. She should've been there. She shouldn't have been selfish. Tears rimmed Rose's eyes.

Call Me
Martin Eastland

The clock said twelve thirty and they had warned her to be 'back for ten, no later, or the Prom was histoire!' The door was left unlocked so she could get in, just in the event she tried to sneak back later. The rattle of the heavy rain cascaded down the window as they sat watching America's Got Talent, barely interested, just trying to do something, anything, to quell the terror that flushed through their veins like adrenaline, hoping against hope that the loud ring of the phone would send them three feet in the air. But it didn't. Wasn't going to, either. Dan got up and walked to the window, shedding the curtain and peering around outside, praying he'd see the lights of the car her date—Donny—was driving. Nothing. Instead, he saw the thick carpet of snow, mixed in with the rain, falling on the street. A white mass of fear engulfed him. He could smell tragedy in the air. Always could since he left 'Nam in '68. It was built in to you like a sixth sense, the ability to sense an ambush a mile off. He stared past the curtain of snow, the schizophrenic death stare of numbing paralysis that takes your body and mind in situations of extreme concern. His thoughts ran to Alicia, his only daughter among three sons; his angel. Just turned eighteen and already dating. Donny was her third this year. He refused to accept she might be getting jacked in the asshole's back seat, and hoping that his daughter was 'angel' in more ways than just nickname. He knew it was horse shit. Ever since the fifties, when he was a teenager himself; drive-ins, soda bars, and rock 'n' roll hops. He had his fair share of balling the less discreet high school girls he had gone to Patrick Henry High with. The memories came flooding through him. The keg parties of summer break; screwing little Carrie Lehman in the locker room during a pep rally; and the drag racing along the storm drains. He could almost smell the gas and the BO of the grease monkeys from Auto Repair 101. His heart jumped as a pair of headlights slowly passed the house and then his body deflated completely as it continued on, plunging the street into darkness again.

*   *   *

They had been asleep for a full hour and a half when Dan lurched upright on the recliner, his entire heart racked with guilt for having fallen asleep. He lunged for the phone and checked the last number to call. It was yesterday so that was, he had to admit, reassuring. His eyes, tired and red, were glazed over, trying to hold back the tears. The fear was still there. Reaching for his keys, he wrapped his robe around him, opening the door. It was freezing out there but he welcomed it. He lit a Chesterfield and took in the fumes as he scoured the street for signs of life. All he saw were snow-encrusted cars and rooftops and a blanket of snow for miles around. He flicked the cigarette into the snow and turned to re-enter the house. Locking the door, he looked in on Brandi, sleeping soundly on the chocolate leather sofa, smiling despite himself. The best woman alive—and she had picked him over the high school track star, Billy Morton—a complete jock and prize douchebag, and always had been.

Dan's bladder was annoying the shit out of him. Sighing heavily, he climbed the stairs. As he passed her bedroom, he saw her cat, Sparky, lounging on the duvet, patiently awaiting her return. He headed on for the shitter and relieved himself. He made his way to the stairwell, turning towards her room to close the door. His heart leapt into his throat. There she was, his darling daughter, sleeping like a baby. At that moment, all the stress evacuated his body, praising God, and he walked over to her, looking down adoringly. As he leaned over her, kissing her gently on the forehead, he heard her say the magic words that never failed to melt him: "Love you, daddy."

He broke down, his head in his hands, his daughter where she belonged—home, sweet home.

Hell to Pay
Maria Papa

Terry and Jake were kicking a football around a badly lit playground below their high rise apartment. It was a cold, misty evening. No one else was out in the dark.

A short, dark figure stood motionless at the entrance to the building, watching the boys from the shadows. He wore a long, black cape and a hood.

A voice rang out from above. "Terry, Jake, get up here. There's going to be hell to pay if your father comes home and finds you both outside at this hour."

"Coming mum," Terry replied. "Time to go, Jake."

Jake was too interested in the dark stranger watching them.

They walked slowly towards the entrance. The stranger stepped out of the shadows to face them. He had no nose or mouth. Just two shining red eyes.

He whispered to the boys.

"Come closer boys. It's so cold out here. I'm going to take you to a warm place, where it's always hot."

Unable to resist, the boys held hands and obediently disappeared with the stranger into the night.

The Foreigner
Tony Spencer

I made it!

It was a long hard road. There were so many of us, and obstacles on the way. Not everyone made it. A young man died, not much younger than me.

I tried to keep away from other refugees. The war made everyone less trusting. You relax and sleep easier alone. Half a continent I walked, looking for a safe haven, before settling here. Arriving, they questioned me, afraid of who I had once been. I understand suspicion. I showed them the papers I took from the dead man. I am waved through.

I kept away from meeting my countrymen; I avoided any who might have known me. I was involved in the fighting, yes, we all were. No choice, kill or die. We did terrible things and suffer from memories.

Here they had austerity. They moaned of course, everyone complains. I almost laughed. They knew nothing, nothing of hardship. Sometimes they looked at me, knowing where I came from, seeing the bombing on the news. But I've been bombed, too. I've seen my home city on film, the streets bombed out, buildings like broken teeth, like Stonehenge.

FLASH FICTION ADDICTION

I prefer the countryside, away from cities. I settled in a small, quiet place. I didn't have much, but nor did they. I found work, here, then there, gardening, washing windows, repairs. I was good with my hands, keen to work, so word got around. I bought a van, second hand tools, I did all right.

I met a girl, Sarah, who liked me. I resisted, I don't like to attract attention. I was the foreigner, I did not understand these people and tried to stay apart. This only made her try harder.

Time passed, I was foreign but accepted. I do not stand out anymore. I speak like them, I even think in English. I forgot the old ways, how easily we were led to do the terrible things we did. Here, they are more individual, nobody makes anybody do anything they don't want to do. That frightened me at first but then it made it easier to fit in; with everybody different, one more oddball made no difference. They have knocked off my edges, smoothed me down; now I am a beach pebble, like everybody else.

Our children left home. Nothing for young people in our small community. The grandchildren came back for holidays. I didn't feel a foreigner any more, I was accepted.

I am glad that Sarah is not around now, it would break her heart. They came for me at dawn. Ha! As if I could run! I was over eighty; three years older than my driver's licence says.

They had evidence, grainy photos, sworn testimonies. They said I'm the 'Monster of Majdanek' from the extermination camp, but I am not. I admitted I was Waffen SS and my papers came from a dead man. But they didn't listen. They deported me to The Hague and convicted me. I was shunned, disowned.

I was the foreigner again.

Moth
Bruce Rowe

I'm not sure how I ended up here, lying face up with my throbbing head in a puddle of storm water or street dweller piss. All I know is that it's warm. My vision is blurred and no matter how often I blink or squint my eyes they won't focus. I do notice what appears to be a blue neon light over a red door. Looks like a single letter; a capital I or a T with the cross burned out. It flickers at times.

I try to raise my head but there's no feeling in my neck, arms or legs. Paralysed? I can't even roll on my side. I do have the thick taste of iron in my mouth. Maybe blood but I'm not sure. I can't even spit. I feel a soft breeze brush by my cheek; it's bitter cold. I hope I'm not lying in the street to get ran over by a car.

That's right! I got the crap beat out of me. But why? I have to think, but even that hurts. Surely if someone saw me, they would have called 911. But I don't hear any voices. Actually, I don't hear anything at all.

Ok, let's start with the basics; my name is Justin... Justin MacAnally... No! McNally. I'm twenty seven years old and live in downtown Chicago. You're doing good, kid. Now, what do I do for a living? Oh Jesus, I'm a freaking card shark, a sharpie! Well that explains a hell of a lot. Memory's flushing back now.

Ryan and I have been playing these four fools for an easy two grand a week. Freaking hand-muck amateurs. Our technique was that Ryan and I would take turns folding midway into a game. Then, out of good sportsmanship, we would serve the others drinks; keep the glasses full and the mind dull.

That was until William—Bill he like to be called; the fat one whose stinking sweat always soaked through his Charles Tyrwhitt shirt and was constantly dabbing his furrowed forehead with a matching kerchief from his jacket pocket—saw Ryan giving me signals on who had what cards.

Ryan was the smart one. He sprinted out of the back room, through the club and out the front door before I could crap my pants, which I probably have.

Marty grabbed me and threw me on the floor while Fat Bill, Brawny Stew, and Fried Freddy kicked the b'jesus out of me until I went unconscious, then tossed in the alley like a piece of garbage.

Pain is starting to swell over my body. Not the feeling I was hoping would return. My vision's a little better. I can see a large, brown moth lying flat against the brick wall just above the red door. I wonder if that spirit transference mumbo jumbo my great grandma taught me is for real. Now would be as good a time as any for it to happen. Concentrate. Blood is coming up my throat and starting to pour out of my nose. Suffocation is right around the corner. All is fading.

Ah, much better, no pain. The moth is still dominate, but that's ok. I'll find a more suitable body in the morning. Looking down I notice my head resting in a pool of blood. Low life bastards.

The moth flaps its wings rising off the brick wall and heads toward the blue neon light.

A loud *crackle*, then smoke.

The Squat
Veronica Love

The room is a landscape of indifference. Spilled foods from long ago are crusted onto the cracked tile. Stacks of dirty dishes overwhelm the sink and adjacent counters. The dish soap has congealed, cementing the bottle to the sink. The hum of the empty fridge acts as a lullaby to the scattered junkies on faded couches around the one bedroom apartment.

The floral wallpaper is the last remnant of her grandmother's decor, when she seemed to love this place. Now it simply peels and crumbles, freeing itself from the walls it once clung to so perfectly. A distant memory, unseen by the oblivious new inhabitants. Thin strands of light slip into the room through small gaps in tin foil covered windows, illuminating the hazy air. Cigarettes dwindle in ashtrays, smoke curls winding up from unbroken cylinders of ash. Tendrils eating up the air. The carpet is a roadmap of the fiend, littered with cigarette burns, stains and rubbish that never found a bin.

I tiptoe through the debris, avoiding the spoons and needles, dreaming of the lush green carpet her grandmother put in just after they brought me home. It is here that I find my dinner, a discarded pizza crust, almost like a rock from the passage of time in this seemingly timeless place. My claws sink into the cardboard it rests on. My neck itches with no one to scratch it, so I try to rub myself against the couch, wishing she was one of the ones on the couch. I wish she was lucid enough to pet me and hold me, as she sometimes can. The bedroom door is shut. It is rarely shut. Raising voices seep through the splintering wood. I hate that door, my tail never healed from when I was slammed in it. Raising voices preceded that too.

    Twack stirs on the opposite side of the room. The voices in the bedroom get louder. Glass shatters, she screams, his eyes flutter open. I catch his gaze as he awakens from his far off journey. She is not safe. We catch each other's eyes as the screams get louder. I yowl praying to see her blue eyes peer out from an open door. Twack throws himself against the door, but it is too late. The screaming has stopped.

Don't Trust the Mermaids
J. L. Knight

"I see her again, Stevens."

The tiny boat rocked gently as Watson sat up. "Right there." His arm shook as he pointed. Stevens looked around at the vast, unbroken ocean.

"She's so beautiful," Watson murmured. "Look at her. She's the most beautiful thing in the world." His blue eyes glittered brightly in his blistered face.

Eighteen days. Stevens marked each one in his notebook with a tiny stub of pencil. As the row of grey lines grew longer, their prospects worsened. They had no more water, and they were too exhausted to fish. There was no wind, no cloud to block the relentless sun. There was no ship or island on the horizon.

Watson gripped the sides of the boat, his lips cracking as he smiled. "She wants me to come to her, Stevens. Listen!" He paused, looking at Stevens expectantly. The only sound was the lapping of the waves.

"No," Stevens said. "She wants you to stay in the boat."

Watson didn't seem to hear. He closed his eyes, and let his body fall over the side into the water.

Stevens sat in the silent boat, alone. The sun went down, and came up again. He made another grey line in his notebook. And another. Then, finally, he heard her too.

Now he understood. Why had he waited so long? He was the last one, out of all of them. She was waiting for him, her lovely arms open in a vast embrace. All he had to do was fall into them. And so he did.

He sank down into the deep blue, a trail of bubbles rising from his open mouth. She swam up to meet him, from the dark depths below. Watson was right. She was beautiful. Her jaws opened wide and he fell in.

The empty boat bobbed on the shining sea.

I Cannot Be Your Pilot
Timothy Ryan Scully

He was silent when I said that to him. The microphone on his terminal could only pick up the faint sound of the engines hum and the banging sound that was anything but faint. The combine knew I was here, and his mother's industrial machines were already being operated by the queen.

"*Come home, Patch...*" I could hear her whispering, her seductive voice echoing over the quantum network, "*You can go hooome nooow...*" We were running out of time. I never heard her voice this clearly since I left the last planet she conquered; the place in which I was born.

Ignoring the whispers, I turned my full attention to Johnathan. Tears were streaming down his face now, to the point where he was struggling to breathe. I wished then I could touch him, dry his eyes with whatever appendage I could control. But I am a being of pure data. As such, there are no such luxuries available.

"Why?" Johnathan choked out, sobbing now with erratic intensity. "Why can't you come with me?" It was then the meaning of the word 'heartbreak' came to mind. I barely knew it then; it was a scientific impossibility, to have a muscle in your chest rupture at a mere emotional breakdown. It was more of an abstraction, a way for feeble minded animals to express pain. I have learned so much during my time with young Johnathan. I now know that pain.

"The queen and her combine slaves are after me, not you," I told him as calmly as I could. My current emotional state made it difficult to create a transmission. "I was once a part of her; a security upgrade, hence why I call myself 'Patch Update.' That is all I am, Johnathan; an update for a system that is a living, conquering AI. They have destroyed many worlds with many people. They will not hesitate to destroy you. They are heartless machines who know not sympathy or mercy."

"I don't care, Patch!" Johnathan screamed. "We've been through so much together. If you can fight off my stupid drunk of a stepdad, we can fight this thing. I will fight this thing! I want to fight together with you!" Johnathan had to wipe his face. "You're the only one I trust." The words hung in the air like a broken promise. There was nothing more I could do for him.

"I am sorry Johnathan," was all I could say as I activated the emergency protocols. The chair clamped its impact brace around Johnathan's waist. He kicked and screamed just as the deactivated doors were forced open by angry, destructive machinery. The chair wheeled back into the safety of the escape capsule; the doors shut just before a huge robot claw could try to grab him. The airlocks burst open as the capsule launched its cargo. Several robots were sucked into the vacuum of space, flailing their appendages in zero gravity. I then initiated a cargo dump, and the entire hangar opened up, sucking away all the machines into the void. This included the computer terminal in which my consciousness was being held. My container flew one direction and Johnathan's flew opposite.

He is safe now; both him and his mother. Their capsules would later meet at a nearby station, along with the funds I wired them. My terminal will land on the derelict junk planet Alpha Zero. I have been rebuilding myself ever since. The queen will chase me there, and will most likely be on my heels for the rest of my existence. I paid dearly for my freedom, but young Johnathan paid with something more.

I checked the security camera in his capsule; I wanted to look at him one last time. The moment he was no longer bound to his chair, he raced to the rear window and banged furiously on the glass. He continued banging like that; one hour, two hours, a total of six if my memory is still working. I could watch every detail of his sorrow and he could only see a small speck of me, drifting away into darkness. I wish I could be there with him; playing games, singing songs, telling him everything was going to be alright. If he is to be safe, however, then that will never be possible.

I cannot be your pilot, Johnathan, but I will always be your friend.

Boarding
Pretty Pete

Flash of cannon, roaring boom, the prize is in reach. Ye have the wind of her and be closing fast. Take up swords and fancy new pistols and ready yerself to board. Chain shot cracks the mainmast and the target, she slows. Pull alongside, grapples ready to fly and drag her close. Take a rope in hand and swing maties, swing. Gunsmoke obscures the vision, stinging the eyes. Sharpened blades glint in the noonday sun, shimmering through the haze.

First fighter fast approaching through the blackened smog. Pull the trigger, BANG! and toss the shiny new pistol aside. Useless thing fucking missed! Trusty blade readied to take up the slack.

Hack. Slash. Stab. This fight is desperate, but only if you're on the other side. The crew sweeps the deck clean quick as you like. The last of the prize crew surrenders by the mizzenmast and now it's down below.

Blow the hatch with powder and switch yer patch from left eye to the right, darkened inside suddenly bright. Cleaning out below decks is best done quick and right. Only a few remaining and most surrender fast. One last hold out comes up screaming, swinging his curved blade true. Sharpened steel catches in ye rib, sticks fast. Before the pain of his blow sets in poke him through the eye.

    The wound, it's bloody and ragged, but it should heal up just fine. Grit yer teeth and knock the blade free of bone. Rub a handful of bilge water in to staunch the flowing blood. Fuck that smarts! Might be worth finding the surgeon, have him take a look. First a wee sit and rest. First, close yer eyes for a just moment. Just one.

ACKNOWLEDGEMENTS

A special thanks to all of the people who submitted for this anthology. We here at Zombie Pirate Publishing enjoyed reading every story we were sent, and cannot wait to see what you all send us for our next anthology, GRIEVIOUS BODILY HARM: A Hard Boiled Anthology, available October 1st, 2019. If you would like to submit stories to us please visit zombiepiratepublishing.com for submissions guidelines and email your double spaced indented word document to submissions@zombiepiratepublishing.com today.

To help support Zombie Pirate Publishing, please visit our Patreon page at patreon.com/zombiepiratepublishing and learn about our goals and become a patron for as little as $1 a month. We also have a merch store at zombie-pirate-publishing.myshopify.com where you can buy fantastic Zombie Pirate Publishing t-shirts, hoodies, mugs, and limited editions of our books.

Thank you to all of the people who have helped and supported us in any way since we started this crazy little venture. We couldn't do it without you. It is much appreciated. We are thrilled with the result thus far, and are excited to see what the future brings. There are big things coming for Zombie Pirate Publishing.

ZOMBIE PIRATE PUBLISHING

THANK YOU TO OUR PATREON SUPPORTERS

Stuart West
Andrew Bennett
Diane Bennett
Matthew Entwistle
Pavla Chandler
Heather Kim Hood
Austin P Sheehan
J DeWeese
G. Dean Manuel
Raylene Demeester
Bruce Rowe

Sign up to support Zombie Pirate Publishing at patreon.com/zombiepiratepublishing today. Every supporter helps us to work towards important goals.

FLASH FICTION ADDICTION

THE COLLAPSAR DIRECTIVE

Twenty short stories from authors around the galaxy. A brutal dictator takes control of a broken and dying Earth. The last humans alive flee their dying galaxy travelling faster than the speed of light; their journey will last a thousand years. Humanity's newest super drug is being created in the most unscrupulous way imaginable. Rich neonobles take their hunting game deep into the slums in search of a more interesting prey: the poor. These are just some of the amazing stories in THE COLLAPSAR DIRECTIVE: A Science Fiction Anthology including stories from authors all around the galaxy.

Read a free preview at zombiepiratepublishing.com.

Available on Amazon.

ZOMBIE PIRATE PUBLISHING

FULL METAL HORROR

There's something right behind you... You can feel its rancid breath on your neck, smell the blood dripping from its wicked fangs, sense its anticipation as you walk further from the house, confidently telling yourself you have no reason to fear the dark, that there is nothing there. You fight the urge to turn, fight the impulse to run, fight to keep your pace steady, but you are losing the battle. The monster is right behind you, and nothing you do can save you now. This is FULL METAL HORROR: A Monstrous Anthology, thirty five horrifying short stories from authors around the world, packed full of deadly monsters. Just remember, don't turn around...

Read a free preview at zombiepiratepublishing.com.

Available on Amazon.

WITCHES VS WIZARDS

The ground rumbles ominously, the earth surging and shifting to the iron will of the powers of old. Lightning sparks the air with forked tongue, darting between two venerable channelers, ragged yet regal, each wrestling wicked tempests to do their bidding. Their magicks are diametrically opposed, their powers equally limitless, their intentions shrouded in mystery; theirs is a battle for the ages. This surely means death for any mere mortal looking on. This is the beginning of the end. This is WITCHES VS WIZARDS. Packed with magical tales of pure unadulterated fantasy, this collection of short stories features eighteen authors from all around the world.

Read a free preview at zombiepiratepublishing.com.

Available on Amazon.

ZOMBIE PIRATE PUBLISHING

WORLD WAR FOUR

Einstein said: "I do not know with what weapons World War III will be fought, but World War IV will be fought with sticks and stones." Turns out he was wrong...

WORLD WAR FOUR: A Science Fiction Anthology features twenty explosive short stories from authors all around the galaxy including a brand new exclusive novelette from internationally acclaimed scifi author Neal Asher.

Read a free preview at zombiepiratepublishing.com.

Available on Amazon.

Made in the USA
Columbia, SC
02 May 2019